PROBABILITIES

by
MICHAEL STEIN

THE PERMANENT PRESS
Sag Harbor, New York 11963

For Hester

ACKNOWLEDGMENTS

Thanks to Robert Boorstin, Joseph Finder, David Porter, Michele Souda, and Paul Spector for their insights and suggestions. And to Hester, whose writing inspires me.

Copyright © 1995 by Michael Stein

Library of Congress Cataloging-in-Publication Data

Stein, Michael, 1960–
    Probabilities / by Michael Stein.
        p.   cm.
    ISBN 1-877946-57-5 : $22.00
    I. Title.
    PS3569.T3726P76   1995
    813'.54—dc20   94-11558
                                CIP

first edition: 1500, August 1995

Manufactured in the United States of America

THE PERMANENT PRESS
Noyac Road
Sag Harbor, NY 11963

CHAPTER 1

Of course I was interested in seeing the dogs. But in truth, I was more interested in seeing the shooting, that is, the shooting of the dogs. After all the movies, TV, videos, everyone is curious to see the thing live, then dead, bullet entry and exit and all that. Not that I'm vicious, but Dr. Kuhn invited me.

I never knew how long they would last, men like Dr. Kuhn, how long until the performance was spoiled and my mother's unnaturally steady mood was again upset. So I took the intriguing offers I was given.

My mother had driven me over to Bergenville General to meet the good doctor, her newest admirer, at his place of business. On the way, she mentioned that he was a bachelor and not a widower or divorcee like most of her admirers were. I don't know where she found those guys, maybe at work, or through friends or in supermarkets. I don't know where she found the doctor, but his being a bachelor made him questionable and a little sleazy to my thinking; what had he been doing his whole life? Judging by her evenings away from home, I assumed she had been seeing this Dr. Kuhn for about three weeks.

We took Mountain Avenue up to the tidy brick hospital entrance, and when we pulled up the drive to the ER she parked where the sign read 'NO STANDING,' and said to me, "Well, at least it doesn't say 'NO PARKING.' We won't get a ticket anyway. I have connections." The ambulances in front of us sounded like a video-game arcade. EMTs were jumping out the back doors, pumping on chests, saving lives, doing their life and death tricks, tubing hanging out of their back pockets. It gave me gooseflesh to watch the stretchers sliding into the darkness of the hospital. Hospitals had scared me since my father went into one and didn't come out. They

3

filled me with pity and interest and made me determined to stay well forever. Sick people made me think about myself.

We got out of the car and went inside through the power-sliding doors that popped open like a swimmer coming up for air. The place stank of cigarettes and bad fish, and my mother left me sitting in an orange plastic chair designed for the curved back of an 80-year-old while she made her way to the front desk. Around me, the sick (as opposed to the very sick who had already passed into the exam rooms) were slobbering and hissing and making ridiculous sounds, and I stared at a girl of about ten doing cartwheels right on the gray carpeting. I was sure she was going to crack some ribs.

At the front desk, I saw my mother put her purse up next to the clipboards with the chained pencils, lean over and say something to the receptionist whose face glowed green from her computer screen. The woman smiled, turned her mouth to a microphone, and I heard, "Dr. Kuhn to the waiting area. Dr Kuhn. Dr. Kuhn to the waiting area." A moment later, the door to the actual emergency room itself swung open and a man about twenty years younger than my mother came out in a scrub shirt and bloody moccasins, signaling for us to follow him. He had a big grin and wore his stethoscope like a tie, and the first thing I thought was: Jesus, what does a guy that young see in my mother? We went into the patient area a few steps behind him.

There was a small group of medically dressed people ahead of me, and to my left and right, stretchers, like boats docked for refueling, were partially revealed behind a blue curtain that ran from ceiling to ankle height. Closest to the doctors and nurses there was a man tied by his wrists with cheesecloth to the railings of his stretcher. The sheet he was supposed to be on was sliding off to one side so he was lying on a plain black foam mattress, the yellow stuffing popping out at the corners. There was an old-sneaker smell coming from him. He had a bloody scab over his left eye and his lip was split. He looked across at a doctor in front of me who was writing a note, and yelled, "Hey baldy!" The doctor looked over at him briefly and returned to his writing. Then the stretcher man yelled, "Hey baldy. Who's the bitch with the brooch?" The doctor writing looked up again, turned around, saw us, stood and came over to us. He gave my mother a kiss and said to me, "Welcome to the Inn, son."

So it wasn't the young guy. This guy, baldy, was Dr. Kuhn. He was smaller than I was, maybe five foot six, with a thick chest and sharp blue eyes. He wore a hyper bow tie that was red and pink and I suppose was hypnotizing for the sick.

"How often do you do surgery?" I asked.

"When it's needed."

"Could you get me a gallstone on your next trip in?" It was one of those things that I'd always wanted to see.

"What do you want with a gallstone, son?"

"I want to start a necklace for my girlfriend," I told him.

My mother whispered, jerking her head at me, "He doesn't have a girlfriend." In a sense she was right and in a sense wrong.

"You want a calcium or cholesterol stone?" he asked me. There were beeping, whining machines rolling past us, as we stood there in the middle of the room on the shining tiles.

"Whatever," I said. "Any interesting cases in here today?"

He motioned for me to talk softer.

"Behind that curtain is a man who tried to kill himself for the third time this year," he said. "Tried to shoot himself and missed again. Actually got a piece of one ear, so he needed some stitching. Behind that curtain is a gal with a seizure. And of course you see Roger over there." He pointed to my friend with the cheesecloth handcuffs.

Then he asked me one. "You ever do any hunting, son?" which was the third time he called me that. Although he had come out looking generous from the gallstone discussion, I gave him a look that meant: Don't call me son, I'm nothing of the sort to you.

"No," I said.

"You've never been hunting in Bergenville?" He seemed surprised.

You have to understand that our town is an ordinary suburb, about as wild as folded linen, that our idea of a forest is a redwood patio deck. I suppose if you stood in the middle of the basketball courts at Tryon Park and took a slingshot to a few seagulls who were lost inland, that could be considered hunting.

I had already said "No" once and I saw no reason to repeat myself.

"Well it just so happens," he said, "that along with chipmunks, squirrels, and rabbits, there is a pack of wild dogs living here."

"Where?" I asked, now mildly interested.

"On the East Side."

I had forgotten that beyond the grand homes on Pam Street there was a little tree density backing onto the golf course and the Palisades.

"Oh yeah?" I said, not giving him much since I could tell he was taunting me. It was his personality.

My mother stood watching us with a little bit of a smirk and a little bit of a smile, arms crossed, not sure what to make of us, but hoping that it was going well. She had on her purple floral dress and a coral necklace. You could see the moles on her chest.

"They're called coy-dogs," he said.

"Coy-dogs."

"A mixture of coyote and dog."

"That's crazy," my mother broke in. She usually let me meet her men friends in this way, allowing us to have our own conversations.

"My dear girl," he said to her, "it's crazy only if they don't come into your backyard and growl at your dog, only if they don't follow you when you're out for an evening walk."

He called me "son" and her "girl," which probably wasn't getting him any points with either of us. He thought he was the coy dog.

"You're making the whole thing up," I said. "Coy-dogs. Come on. They're probably just some undernourished shepherds out on the town."

"A mauled Canada goose was found last night near Winchester Pond. I believe the coy-dogs are responsible," he told us.

"You're not going to shoot them, are you?" my mother asked.

He ignored this question. "In fact, I've been asked by the

town council to capture them. My next-door neighbor is on the council. She's very competent. I had never heard of the problem, but when I did, naturally I offered my services."

"Why even bother with them?" my mother asked. She took off her pink frame glasses, and let them hang from her neck on a thin pink strap. When her glasses came off it meant that she was concerned.

"We have concluded that the dogs are a hazard."

"You're not going to shoot them," she said, this time a bit hesitantly.

"You have to think of the safety of children."

Then I knew what was what. Once the old packaging— "the safety of children"—came up, gross torture of the animals would be next on the agenda.

"I bet the people reporting this haven't seen any wild dogs, only wild children," I said, trying to lighten things up a bit.

It didn't work. "The Animal Shelter has failed to control them with traps. They say the adult dogs won't go near the traps, they're too smart, and all they've caught are a dozen puppies." He was serious about his mission. It troubled me that this healer would be out there killing puppies. His hands were down at his sides, but now they met in front of his belt and started squeezing, pumping, like a heart.

"Many people support us."

"So you're going to shoot them," I said. I have never much followed my mother's line of thinking, but this was an exception. She seemed on the right track. Of course the difference between us was that I wanted to see the shooting and she would want nothing to do with it.

"Many people support us."

I realized he still hadn't really answered the question, just like every doctor I'd ever met, and this question wasn't even about doctoring. But of course he had answered it, with the "safety of children" line.

"I'd like your son to join me on the hunt. I am going out with two animal control specialists."

She looked right at him and said, "Absolutely not." My mother is actually pretty tough sometimes.

"He will be paid $200 for each dog captured."

I said, "Absolutely."

"He will not be allowed to go hunting."

I just stood there and watched. She had just rooked me out of 200 big ones or up. There was no point in whining, though. Wouldn't work and it wasn't my style. Plus, I was interested in watching my mother in this conflict. Always a pleasure to see her disagreeing with one of her admirers.

Then he looked at me. "The hunt is tomorrow morning. Seven A.M."

I wasn't sure what he meant by giving me the exact time. And most Saturdays I left town anyway. But I thought that I'd stay around and see what happened. He gave my mother another kiss, as if to say, "Back to work now," although this time she gave him only her right cheek. The drunk on the stretcher called out, "Hey honey, tell baldy to shut up, and you come over here and help me with this itch."

At home that night, I took up Dr. Kuhn's case. First because I wanted to go and second because it was a good chance to shake up my mother some.

I said to her, as she served her six-minute specialty, flounder baked with a can of vegetarian vegetable soup on top, "Don't you believe in the public welfare?"

The edges of the fish were brown and the veggies slopped onto the aluminum foil that lined the pan. It was like I had just woken her up; she had no idea what I was referring to. "Like rabies. Like the dogs will get infected and spread the disease to people."

"It's ridiculous. No one has been attacked."

"You have to think of the safety of children . . . and pets," I said. It was revolting but I said it, adding "pets" to make it more revolting.

"You are not going out shooting guns."

"Think of the negative impact on our wildlife."

"No guns."

I don't remember much about what else happened that evening anymore. I think I stayed in and watched basketball on TV and fiddled with a few equations. I'd been thinking about the old Monte Hall problem, the three-curtain problem, where some hysterical woman contestant was offered her choice of three curtains, only one of which had a real prize behind it, the other two giving away bogus items like ceiling fans or wooden legs. Monte stood there after she made her choice and, depending on her pick, offered her maybe a thousand dollars instead of her curtain. She stood there uncertain as could be, looking at the ten hundred-dollar bills in his hand under her nose and struggling with a real-life probability problem. If he was offering money she must be on the right track; or was he tricking her? Should she switch her pick? The solution to the problem was actually quite complex, and our math class had been working on it extra hours like some kids would go out and do grounder practice. The poor sucker on TV had no clue how to think it through so she just guessed and usually ended up with audience sympathy and a prosthesis.

I keep track of my mother's men friends by matching them to probability problems I'm working on at the time I meet them. For instance, Monte's three curtains, Dr. Kuhn's ER curtains.

My mother had a different voice when she was around one of the men who had passed through our life in the past two years. It was a lesser-intensity voice, almost like a young girl's, almost baby talk. She had that voice, and she was cheerful and reasonable when she was distracted by her dating. She left me alone. My mother wasn't exactly husband-hunting; she was a realist and silly dreams didn't enter into her assessments of men. But she had this urgent need to think of herself in terms of who she was with, manwise, and although she knew this was ridiculous, I believe she did not know how else to think of herself. She didn't long for a life different from what she had—that was too complicated—she just liked company.

After one man disappeared and before another showed up, and if I couldn't escape quickly enough when I saw her coming, she would rant about "men" to me. They were impossible, cruel, hysterical, they expected to be taken care of ("when I have a son to look after," she'd throw in), they made promises and spent too little, they were moody, bossy, bad dancers, they reeked of cheap cologne. They had been single so long they had forgotten how to treat women.

When I overheard her talking to herself she would say, "The thing is not to care," or "Don't expect too much," or

"You don't need that kind of company." "I have more energy than they do," was her most common complaint and I had no doubt about it. Some of them were old men, just a belt and a head. For a woman in her 50s who was a little overweight, she never stopped moving. She couldn't even sit through a whole meal; she always cleared away my plate before I was finished.

She, her newest man, and me always made a strange mix when we first met. She had roles for all of us, of course. I was meant to be her pet and also some sort of protection for her, a high-school-aged representation of her responsibilities; the man was an insider, the new confidant, but also a stranger; she was the centerpiece, the excuse for all this fun, the main attraction.

At 6:45 A.M. the next morning, Dr. Kuhn's black Mercedes convertible parked in front of our house. My mother and I were both up, edgy, retreating from conversation. I watched through the window as he got out in his camouflage khakis, duck hunter hat, lace-up black boots.

"Hunting season," I said back over my shoulder.

The knocker sounded on the front door. My mother stayed on her seat in the kitchen and I went for the good doctor. He was opening and closing his fists when I opened the door.

"Morning," he said to me in passing, and then he was by me like he knew where to find her.

He went past the stairs, probably following the smell of toast. He had never been to our house as far as I knew.

"On your left," I yelled after him. I stayed where I was.

"I'm going to take your son hunting," he said to her in the kitchen.

"I've asked you not to," she said quietly.

"He's old enough to decide for himself," he said.

"I disagree." This was not very sophisticated of her to say with me in hearing range.

"I'll take you two out to dinner tonight," he said.

"I don't think so." I didn't know why she was mad at him.

As he turned from her, I could hear the squeak of his boots, and he was back next to me a second later.

"How are you feeling, son?"

"Life's always a surprise."

"Never plan ahead," he said. "I don't even buy green bananas anymore. Let's go."

I had on Converse hightops, jeans, and a black turtleneck. I threw on a jean jacket. It would have been mean to say "bye" to my mother, so I did.

In his Mercedes he said, "This will be like the War."

"Which war?"

"The Pacific Theater."

I was quiet, and he got the point.

"World War II," he said. I calculated that that made him high 60s. He seemed in good humor. He drove fast, but I'd never been in a Mercedes and it cornered pretty well. He seemed satisfied with his own thoughts so I left him alone. It was a cold day, sunny, with high clouds and a glare. It had been a February with snow that melted quickly. I had the feeling that something important would be happening that day. It would be a day that I'd remember.

He had brought a plaid thermos and he offered me some of its contents as he unscrewed the top. When I declined, he poured himself something red, said, "All for one and one for all," and tipped back the plastic cup. His fingers actually looked dainty on the tiny handle.

We drove to the East Side. Beyond the estates, the woods backed onto the golf course on one side and the Palisades on the other, with its drop to the Hudson River, New York City beyond.

"What do you like to do?" he asked as we were about to come to a stop.

"I like math," I told him. "Probability." I figured he was an educated man and would himself have an interest in probability.

"Never studied it. A lacking I suppose, but never stopped me." He turned off the motor and electronically unlocked my door.

"How will we hunt them?"

"It won't be hard."

"How do you know they're here?"

He didn't answer me.

We got out of the car at the end of the dead end, the trees

in front of us. He was walking fast and I noticed for the first time that he was bowlegged. That's when I heard the choppers overhead. And then I noticed a jeep pull up behind us, its cargo area a cage. I thought of my mother for a moment and wondered why she didn't want me to go and I realized how little I knew her in some ways. Two big guys got out of the jeep in blue jumpsuits and farmer's caps but I wasn't given an introduction and that pissed me off. The doctor came back, offered me a rifle, and told me the plan.

It was simple. The two "specialists" would go off into the woods and, with the help of walkie-talkies and the chopper above looking down through the bare trees, would circle the dogs and drive them back toward us. We would walk in a ways, and lie on our bellies hiding in some high brown grass. Then we'd stand up, or he'd stand up, and shoot them. With luck, we'd get them all at one time. One big coy-dog pileup. The doctor was carrying a short black rifle with a thick barrel that the specialists had given him. He also had a belt loaded down with sausage-sized cannisters that held stun-damage in them. It didn't seem hard.

"Do you want your own weapon or not?" he asked one more time.

I told him no. I knew nothing about guns and was worried that I would shoot myself or him by accident in all the excitement. I didn't want to see any blood, I realized. I had no idea about his shooting credentials.

"You're one of those wiseass teenagers, but you don't want to really take responsibility for anything, do you?"

I didn't argue but I felt my face getting red. I really didn't like Dr. Kuhn. He was merciless.

Under the trees the air was brown. I heard birds. We walked in about two hundred yards, him leading, and we lay down, his rifle resting on a tree stump. About six minutes later, I saw them. About fifteen or twenty. They were making scraping noises and were skinny and gray-brown. They looked smaller than I had imagined. They looked quick and brittle among the trees. And they were so close. My spit stopped. I felt my shoulders tighten up.

Dr. Kuhn leveled his gun and fired. I felt its crack inside me. I stared over my forearms and saw a dog shudder and sink, its belly hitting the ground first. A few panicked and ran around in tight circles and the rest just stood still. He reloaded. Another crack and another fell the way the first had, paws spread. The others spun and scattered and as they did, about fifty yards ahead of us I heard other shots and I heard the doctor crack off another few as well. It didn't take more than 90 seconds.

I was biting the sleeve of my coat. It was wet and cold against my lips. I had gooseflesh like the day before at the hospital, thinking of the dogs' new darkness. My mouth tasted of dirt.

Standing, he said, "Gone, goodbye," like the announcers on TV say when a home run is hit. But he said it with a dry laugh. I looked at the stunned dogs, at their doggish and twisted faces, and thought: it doesn't matter. But I felt a little sick and a little guilty for being there. Then I thought of Dr. Kuhn working around illness and I didn't know how to put it next to this. I wondered what my mother saw in the man.

"You should have got one," he said, breathing heavy. "It was great, the bastards dropping so politely like that." I could see his breath. I could see the sweat around the brim of his duck cap. He was pleased with himself.

"I didn't need to," I said.

"It's not need, son. It's want. Have you ever seen anything like that?"

I said I hadn't. He was overexcited.

"It's good work if you don't miss many," he said. Then he said, "That's 600 dollars for me and none for you." That's when I knew I didn't like him. "That's right. That's how the world works. A woman wouldn't have done this job. Your mother couldn't understand what we did here today."

What I wanted to do was hit him. I wanted to see the great doc hunter on the ground. But I didn't.

He drove me home, telling me the rule that the captured dogs would be held for seven days and then put to death unless someone claimed them. As if anyone would claim them.

My mother was an optimist. She tried to see the good side of her admirers (particularly if they had prestigious jobs or were of a higher social category), and blinded herself to most of their faults. When we got home I expected her to just let our morning's adventure pass. But it didn't work out that way. Sometimes she surprised me. Sometimes she held to her own ideas. He must have thought that he could take her on, a man used to having his own way. As my friend Billy said, "There are men who talk to women and men who talk about women," and given the way that Dr. Kuhn spoke of my mother, I put him in the second camp.

He came up to the door with me and my mother opened it before we knocked. She wasn't wearing any lipstick. She looked at him and said, "Thank you," real polite, hooked her hand around my shoulder and pulled me inside, closing the door behind me, right in his face. I knew she wouldn't apologize to me about having liked him. He might never even come up again in our conversation. It hadn't worked out the way she planned. He was gone, that I knew.

Up in my room, on my bed, my brain finally went Whoa! According to probability theory, large effects often have meanings that can't plausibly be explained by chance. What I'm saying is that sometimes you just have to accept the large effects in your life as just that, large effects, and not get all caught up in the whole romantic idea of chance. Of course if you think that mathematics is an invasion from outer space like some of my classmates do, or my mother does, probability theory is hopeless to you. The disappearance of Dr. Kuhn let my mother's hunt continue, and four weeks later she met Lester Warner.

CHAPTER 2

She usually invited her dates in for a drink when they escorted her home and that night was no exception: I heard the two locks click open on the front door and two voices in the living room. Then they crossed in front of the stairs on their way to the kitchen where she took the liquor selection out of the cabinet near the sink and put it on the counter. On a bad night, she poured scotch and soda. On good nights, she poured wine. I washed the dishes usually, so I knew. Most nights, I stayed in my room reading, walked close to the door carrying my book so I could hear them better and only went down to the kitchen if it sounded like they were really having fun and laughing, when I heard the ice music and imagined my mother looking over the rim of her glass at him.

I snuck down, my shirt untucked, pants of the day back on, and without knocking I walked in. The probability that I would *like* any new admirer of my mother's was low, given what I took to be the variables—her history of losers and openness to flattery, my condescension.

When I appeared in the doorway, she asked, "You're still up?" like she was surprised at my sleep pattern after sixteen years with me. Besides, she was usually home from dates by nine, even when they were good, because she felt some responsibility.

"This is my son, Will."

I was already looking at the man and he was looking at me. I waited for him to get up and come over to me with his hand.

"Will Sterling," I said to the man that night in my kitchen, meaning to introduce my dead father's name into the conversation in case my mother had never mentioned it. I turned to my mother. "You got lots of phone calls. Aunt Nina, Hilda, the man who was here last night and the one from the night before that."

15

I was too old to be rude, but it was fun.

She said to her friend, "He's kidding."

"I'm kidding," I said. I checked his expression and saw a trace of a smirk. He kept silent, I kept a straight face. Then I said, "I'm going out now." That always gets her: conflict, for no good reason. She really is very easy to upset when she means to put on a good show.

"Oh no you're not," she said. I had her off-balance. I could tell by the way her foot lifted like she was about to stamp it, and the way it lay down quietly like an old guard dog. My mother had on her purple floral dress, her serious dating dress, and gold earrings like scallop shells. She wore this outfit when she meant to look good. She always said, "Purple brings out the blue in my eyes." The top of her feet looked a little fat coming out of her purple suede shoes, but the belt on her dress was tight and seemed to pull her back in. She had had her hair done that day, auburn.

If one of these men interrupted us before we had finished our dance, I usually wrote him off and began to enjoy the game of making him feel bad. If he sat quietly, I started my interrogation. I asked about his favorite teams, if he had a sweet tooth, what paper he read, usually something to gauge his income. I asked him what the chances were that there would be two triple plays on one day during the major league season to get a sense of his math skills. If she let me go on, I took a step toward him and checked for glass eyes, false teeth, obvious tics or deformities, and with great concern, bracelets and necklaces. My attitude was, and still is, that men at sixty shouldn't have jewelry. I stepped back and if his top button was undone, I checked for hair on his chest, and what color. I hated tasseled shoes.

I turned to her guest that evening and asked, "Where did you go tonight?"

I was not usually so awful but something about these men brought it out in me. They all talked to me in a certain way right off. As if we had some agreed-on loyalty code immediately in place, some masculine let's-be-nice-around-your-mom-although-it's-dishonest routine. I thought that if I burned them with distrust and they recovered, we'd be better off in the long run. I couldn't really understand why they went out with my mother. I had only had a few dates myself, leaving aside the way Sara and me got along and I had to admit that this girl-boy inexperience of mine was slightly retarded for a 16-year-old boy in America. I knew it couldn't be easy for these men to meet me and I could imagine my mother telling them about me, never giving them a clue about my mean streak, but instead playing up my good points and the depth of our good feelings for each other and so on. Setting them up, as it were. But I couldn't help myself around her dates. Terri said I should be kind to them. Terri went so far as to say, "I know you can be sweet if you want to be." She said it hurt my mother if I wasn't.

But that was the point, wasn't it? My mother shouldn't have been out on a school night, a Thursday night, even if I was the one going to school. If she needed to socialize, it should have been with her girlfriends. But it hadn't been like that since my father died.

This man had floppy silver hair, perfect teeth, eyebrows without barbs, blue eyes, a tight belt with a little overlap, the standard blue blazer, two-tone tie, red and blue, and he wore loafers without tassels. Ordinary, nothing fancy. But silver hair with black eyebrows always made a man look sharp.

"Will, this is Mr. Warner."

"What's up with you tonight?" he asked.

What a curious question—most of her dates never asked me anything like this or they smiled and waited for me to excuse myself. Sometimes they offered questions that required short, specific answers, like, What's your favorite subject in school? Or they dishonestly thanked me for allowing them to take my mother someplace that evening. As if it weren't my pleasure. But this unexpected opening was the chance to let him know about us Sterlings. For a moment, I actually thought of telling him the truth. Right out, just like that. The whole dread Will Sterling history, sharing the parts about my mother's disappearing acts over the past few years. How she taught me to keep her company until I was good at it and then she slid off into her other life. But the truth seemed so improbable that it would have scared him as it had scared me from time to time. Telling him the truth also would have made my mother more miserable than I could have tolerated. If he wanted to know, he'd stick around and find out for himself.

"Made dinner. Did the dishes. Read a biography of Cecil Hawkins." I mumbled, making him lean in.

"Hawkins, huh. Better rebounder than scorer." A controversial statement.

"No outside shot," I said. "But he averaged over twenty a couple of seasons."

"No defense in that league." I happened to agree, but since defense was out of style and I had learned from Billy that you should be careful what you say about basketball, I kept quiet. Mr. Warner sounded sure of himself. It made me a little nervous.

"A leaper," I said.

My mother sat there listening. It always surprised me that she could be quiet. When we were alone and I spoke, she interrupted me within eight words. She would say, "Did I tell you . . ." or "Remember I'm leaving in two weeks for . . ." when I was offering her my plans for the weekend. I kept talking right over her when she interrupted. Eventually she got the point and felt ridiculous although sometimes not and then she got angry because I was interrupting her.

"My name's Lester," he said.

I took in the name, seeing what I could do with it. Consonant, vowel, consonant. His parents must have been very orderly, like he was.

"Try not to think about it too much, Will," my mother said. "He tries to think everything through." She said this in an embarrassed way, which was her way of praising me.

"What's going to happen next around here?" I asked.

She laughed in a nutty, drunken way. "Homework?"

I hadn't even started my interrogation.

"See ya," Lester said, and I was gone.

The next morning as I was getting ready for school, she asked, "Well, what did you think?

"About what?"

"About Mr. Warner?"

"Oh, Lester."

"Yes . . ."

"What do you like about him?" I asked her.

This question, offered to her twenty or thirty times since my father died three years ago, made her say the weirdest things, as if I wanted her to be honest with me. Things like, "He looks like my father," or, "He looks like your father," or, "He told me I'm beautiful." Things I shouldn't have had to hear.

It all came from her desperation. My mother had no idea how to date after thirty-two years of marriage, I supposed, and not much hope of finding a man who appreciated 55-year-old women when there were also pretty young things out there looking for gray-haired guys who had earning capacity and good manners. My mother knew this, said this to me, and usually acted like a ridiculous flirt around her boyfriends. Her motives for dating had nothing to do with some sense of duty about getting me a surrogate father. She knew, somewhere past her own needs, that I was too picky to be satisfied. So when she told me what she saw in Lester, I was not really listening. Something about liking his style, I think she said. I knew she was desperate not to live the rest of her life alone.

I was glad it was Friday and I would be leaving the next morning for the weekend.

I made a sandwich for her lunch, made one for myself, wrapped them both in tinfoil, slipped each into a brown paper bag, left one on the counter for her, put my mouth to the kitchen faucet for a quick rinse of the teeth, which was easier than brushing, and headed out the back door.

School was across town. That's about a mile mostly uphill through good neighborhoods. New Jersey in winter is muddy. The back yards were soft that day, my shoes were new, simple brown numbers, bought at a store near where Billy lived that also sold big-heeled red shoes with spikes over each toe. To keep my shoes clean, I took some streets I'd rather have avoided, streets where I might see people I never felt like talking to. The houses on the way were basic, five windows around a door. Like a child would draw. I never drew like that since I preferred squiggles and modern New Jersey schools didn't require conformity. But Terri's kids did drawings like that in Connecticut and their apartment was papered with such garbage. The houses around mine had two cars, the occasional hoop, some brick-eating ivy. The components of the good life were in place on our side of town.

It took me about fifteen minutes to do the mile, about the time of a fast female swimmer over the same distance. I swatted at low branches on the way, patted the bushes shaped into animals at the corner of Queen Anne and Holsworth. I walked on the curb, balancing, wondering if I wanted to do any serious thinking. Such as: I usually skip my third-period class, Spanish, and what I should do with the spare fifty minutes. The new high school report cards had a place for the number of classes missed of each subject. I missed Spanish 37 times last spring and still got an A. That tells you about our school. Once you had a good reputation you could coast, given the dullness of most kids, but one D and you were a marked man for four years. My mother noticed the thirty-seven when I brought the card home, but didn't bother to take the time to figure out what it meant. She asked me, "Thirty seven what?" as she held the onion-skin rectangle for a moment. I said, "The theme of this report card is prime numbers." She looked doubtful but really didn't care. I wasn't flunking. You had to be incredibly stupid or have a drug habit to fail out of my school.

It was not the sort of school the President of the United States would visit in his search for model teenagers. There were no special programs, no inspiring successes, nothing upbeat for the news at six. Besides, the news wasn't interested in math, where Bergenville High School was strong. The local news got anything to do with math wrong, or they fluffed over it if something more than simple addition came up. This one broadcaster on 9 always tried to make it seem like he knew what he was talking about. His top lip didn't move, ever, and he looked particularly lost talking about numbers. I would turn to my friend Billy, if he was over and we were watching the news together, and he'd turn to me and we'd say, "Oops, I left my brain in my other coat pocket," and laugh like crazy. Then Billy usually said, "And he's white too." Billy was the star of the basketball team but he hung around with me anyway. Like me, he was interested in love, but in a different way. When I told him what I did or didn't do with Sara he said, "You're messed up."

But that's the way it was with me and her and me and him. Looking across the football stadium, over the concrete bleachers and the oaks, our high school was a castle with three floors and symmetry, but it was in no way enchanted. At one end was the black door, at the opposite end the white door. These colors meant the type of students who went through them. Most students went in through the center door, passing the principal's office and its sense of order. The toughs came in the sides, black and white "slum children," as that newscaster once said before he disappeared for a month. Except that there were no slums in our town. There were train tracks, like in the most notorious of Southern towns, tracks that separated what might have been slums from what weren't slums, but the black part of Bergenville was just a neighborhood and the white part was just a neighborhood in Bergenville except with different kinds of barbershops. I heard the "slum children" line the night the white police beat on a black kid during an arrest. Then the railroad tracks meant something and the two doors, the black and the white ones at my school, were unpleasant even to pass. Billy lived over there, along with my shoe store. Bergenville was the first town in New Jersey to integrate its schools, teachers were always saying, but we all knew that that was a joke. Still, the administrators were all pleased that it happened here first, and they took credit for it forty years later.

This description should in no way make you despair about my education. I read plenty of books on my own: biographies of mathematicians, sports books, biographies of sports heros. I also read everything I could about teenage girls, forty-year-old women and fifty-five-old women. Sara usually fed me this women's stuff. Her room had the occasional *Elle*, but she and I both preferred firmer material, serious books of the psyche. The general problems of teenage, middle age, and old age didn't seem so dissimilar to me, mostly people fooling themselves, or people who weren't sure about something, but Sara said that I was just a boy, of course I missed the nuances. Occasionally I did try serious literature featuring boys my age. I ended up giving these books away before I read much of them because all the protagonists were truants. I had less use for truants than I did for school.

Sara's room also had lotion bottles, a music stand, a Kleenex box, a framed picture of dancers, an Indonesian basket for earrings, and a nerf basketball hoop I had bought her. The white rug was soft. There was nothing surprising about the room except for the rim and sometimes Sara. Her door had a lock.

I didn't know what I'd do without Sara and still don't.

The rest of my education took place in math class or watching the boys and the few girls who gathered at the black and white doors and just inside, where litter blew in and there were beer stains and it smelled of bad lemons. The black boys tipped around, walking like their knees were giving out. At the other end, the white boys were tighter, making more muscles. It was mostly shouting and pushing and talking about the scum at the other door. Billy said that the difference between the black and white doors was the difference between "Kiss my ass," and "Kick my ass." The funny thing was that the boys from both doors would probably end up in the army together. The few girls who loitered in these scenes smoked and had big hair and fit cozily between their boys' legs. They tried to scare the boys, but they didn't.

My locker was at the black door, my first period was at the white door. Allow me to brag. Most of my white classmates, if they ever found their lockers located near the black door, would have simply moved into the locker of a friend, sharing the six-inch-wide, five-foot-high vertical space. I liked where my locker was. No one bothered me. I played ball and I did math and that was enough for most of the blacks who hung out at the door. When I wanted to show off, I let Billy take me in the black door past them. I had more trouble at the white door where I was not as well known. Plus, the white kids' pushing and playing seemed a little more violent. Some of them, I heard, kicked pregnant women and ate glass.

Fridays went fast. Spanish, third period, was the worst, if I went. In study hall after Spanish, I recuperated from the boredom of conjugations and the hokey, recorded dialogues I was supposed to have memorized in order to improve my accent. I sat in a metal cafeteria chair, the long Formica tables set with books, papers and leaning elbows like a flea market selling teenage debris, and I thought about math class. Lunch the next period was in the same place so I checked the marquee across the room for the menu. I added the prices of the hot dogs and spaghetti and the corn and the french fries and the ice cream and right on down the list, then I added them again coming up. Just to keep in practice. I wondered what Terri would serve for dinner the next night. The day was over at three while I was still digesting.

I usually had math last period and until then there was nothing serious to learn. Math class began with all of us sitting in the back and Mr. Volpo saying, "Hey kid, you're a smart kid, sit here" to the geniuses, gesturing to them to sit up front. They weren't blind, just shy, and preferred to sit in a tight group away from Volpo. I sat with the geniuses out of loyalty. There were only eight of us, accelerated right through calculus, and taught by Volpo. When class ended, I was always slow to leave.

My mother knew where I went on weekends, but never asked questions about the Keans. Or rather, she asked the same question again and again.

"How do you pronounce their last name?"

"Kean, as in clean."

"Irish, huh."

"No, part terrier, part shepherd," I would say, making a joke of Terri and Shep's first names, which she refused to learn.

She knew I was being sarcastic, which is a sixteen-year-old boy's way of ending a conversation. She hadn't bothered to learn the names of any of my friends, except the one or two boys who were particularly polite to her, which I held against them; and when she showed this total lack of interest even in the Keans, whom I saw every weekend unless there was an emergency or money to be made, I would become irritated and put an end to talk. She didn't know Sara's name, but then I never told her about Sara.

"Leave a phone number," she said before she went out for the second night in a row that Friday with Mr. Warner, not expecting to see me the next morning.

There I was, sitting at the kitchen table Saturday morning,

juice in one hand, a yellow number 2 pencil in the other, leaving her the Keans' number as streaks of light and morning noises outside brought me to my senses, when I asked myself the same question I had the two evenings before: What can you be sure of in this life? I viewed this as a probability question, as I viewed most things, and not unlike many my father would ask me, and not at all straightforward. A question with lots of parts to it. My father gave credit for partial solutions to his students and I figured that was the best I could hope for without him. Yes, I was sure I would see the Keans in a few hours, and I was sure that I would see Mr. Lester Warner again, but I didn't have enough information to predict much beyond that. Things I could not put my hands on were changing. All I had was intuition, which, as my father liked to say, was the enemy of probability.

CHAPTER 3

The drive, from one home to another, my mother's to the Keans', took two hours if I left early enough. The roads became narrower, the curves tighter heading north, highways becoming parkways becoming routes and country roads, and I held the wheel less hard passing into Connecticut. My fingers felt puffy and light. The car was my mother's, large and difficult to maneuver, with room for my knees, and power. Six months before, the day after my birthday, I had borrowed a friend's car to pass the driver's exam because I was sure my mother's car would fail me. Because she never asked, she assumed I passed using her Taurus, and so she let me take it whenever I needed. My mother owned another, newer car, also American, steel-reinforced and high off the ground. Her cars got bigger as she grew older. She said that she liked the feeling of safety inside the thick doors. I knew that she traded her cars every two years not because of their "resale value," (that was just a line she had gotten from one of her men friends), but because she wanted the safest car available as suggested by Consumer Reports.

Her cars began to get bigger after my father died. At first, she wouldn't drive at all. She claimed that she didn't like the ice, but after winter melted and she still wasn't driving, she admitted it was something else; bridges. She was afraid to drive over bridges. She said it was the sound of the tires on that open grillwork that scared her. The metallic hum, the singing sound and distant whine, and the thought of the wind beneath her, the cord of water. It worried me also if I thought about it too hard, so I didn't, but my mother couldn't escape her own mind at work. She didn't worry as much though if someone drove her over these bridges. She was able to take the bus to work in New York City without too much of a problem. During the dangerous time, crossing the George Washington Bridge, I told her to count the skyscrapers and think of them as pins in a pincushion. To hide her fear of the bridges, she bought big, solid cars which I suppose reminded her of buses.

For the two years that she did not drive, I walked. I knew every street in Bergenville. I made friends with older kids who drove. I hitched sometimes.

On Saturday mornings I tried to get out of the house before she was up, having said my goodbye for the weekend the night before. When I said good night to her the evening I met Lester Warner I told her, "And for tomorrow too."

"Where are you going tomorrow?" Lester Warner asked.

"Long story," I said. "If dinner gets boring, let my mother tell you." One of his black eyebrows went up.

My mother cleared her throat and then came toward me with her lips for a proper sign-off, but she only got my left ear as I conveniently reached right to turn on the outdoor light. Lester Warner just waved and spared me the firm handshake routine.

It had become a game for me to wake myself without an alarm, to be quiet enough in the kitchen with my cereal, which crunched loudly in my ears, to inch the squeaky folding door of my closet closed, to avoid flushing the toilet, so that she would not come out of her room. If I woke her, I had lost the game and she would inevitably ask me if I had a map, or an extra key, or pajamas, although no sixteen-year-old boy I ever met wore pajamas. She never asked me to reconsider my plans, to hang around for the weekend, or to leave later so we could catch a matinee together.

To avoid her also meant waking up before six A.M. Any later and she padded out in her slippers and heavy blue robe and immediately pulled back the curtains on the kitchen windows, not allowing the half-dark. When I thought of Terri, I thought of how I enjoyed the half-dark, the very early and the before-late, when we usually took our walks.

That day in March there was the long pleasure of the morning and the dips in the road into fog. My arm, resting on the open window, was slightly wet after the first hour. It felt like spring and the moon was still up in the blue sky. At the first toll booth, about thirty minutes in, I always asked the guy taking my change, "Now which way?" which put me in a good mood as I drove on, leaving him confused. About an hour into the trip I started singing. I had a terrible voice that I enjoyed hearing really loud in a closed space. I made up songs about the people in the few cars around me, songs about open liquor bottles and handguns and murder. I was a pessimist on the open road. When I couldn't stand my own melodies, I tried the radio. If I found a typical Saturday morning show on gardening tips or religion, or if I heard music with a heavy bass line I turned it off. Instead, I announced an imaginary basketball game—he crosses to the top of the key, stutters left, pulls up, off the rim, rebound—thinking of Billy's sweet moves or I'd imitate a comedian that I had seen late the night before on TV. Sometimes, I talked to my father. I often talked to him about probability. Genetics is, after all, simply probability played out, so it was natural that I had questions for him. I asked him what he had given me in my character, exactly what been diluted by my mother's contribution. I suppose I got interested in chance under his tutelage. His science books cluttered the basement. His papers were filled with numbers, with cross-outs, equal and unequal signs. In the car I felt the need to confide. I started by talking with my father, but I was really looking forward to seeing Terri so I could confide in her, someone who could actually answer some of my questions.

If I got near the school where the Keans lived much before eight (sometimes this happened when I was in a hurry to escape New Jersey), I slowed down. I knew Terri and Shep would be up because they had little kids, but I didn't want them to think I was pathetic and homeless arriving so early. If it was still before eight when I hit the town next to the school, I stopped at the Waldorf. The Waldorf was a coffee shop stuck between a Ladies' Boutique featuring flat-chested mannequins and a hardware store at the end of the line of stores that made up Grover. It was small and glassed-in, with a long counter split so waitresses could get in and out of the kitchen in back, and there were swivel stools. There were about ten wooden tables and four booths that stared out at the road I would take up to The Winston School. I always sat at the counter. The clock hands would tell me 7:50, no digitals up here.

"Early again," Gert would say, as I sat on the shaky, spinning seat, and put my feet on the gum-infested shelf below. "With or without a donut?" she asked.

"With," I told her, although she knew. Gert hiked her apron, spun, grabbed a cup and a saucer from their piles, put them under the hot chocolate machine. Coffee was only good if there were other people around who would be impressed by my age-to-caffeine ratio.

"Any good accidents?" I said to her back.

"You know the corner past the fresh eggs sign? Last night a car jumped it. They find out the car is stolen from Winston. Wrecked. Jaws of life take the little criminal out from the steering wheel that's torn his nose off. Still blood on the grass, if you look carefully. If you ask me, and nobody does, there's an excess of youth around here," she finished. Gert was no-nonsense, law and order.

"On Tuesday on the Parkway," I told her, "a truck carrying barbecue sauce hit a truck carrying chicken parts. After the fuel burned off, they had a three-lane cookout."

She laughed and I saw her gold teeth like a fighter's hanging there. She put her elbow on the counter in front of me, lifting the top to a see-through cake container so I could nab a jelly.

"What else is new?"

"How were the roads coming up?" she asked me.

"Clear. Quiet. Some construction on 139 but nothing new since last week."

I had been coming to see the Keans for nearly a year on weekends, the first few months by bus until I got my license. Once I drove myself, Gert used me as her alternate route guide for the truckers who stopped in heading south. But mostly farmers came in this early on Saturday. She gave them eye contact and they knew to take a table on their own. She took them coffee, dropped off menus, and came back to her perch near me.

Gert had never met the Keans. They left campus mostly to drop off kids or pick up groceries and the best market was in the town on the far side of the school. They had never been to the Waldorf despite my recommendations. Gert knew I came to visit them, but didn't know much about the school although she had lived her fifty-some years next to it. Never saw a reason to visit. It made no sense to her that I visited a prep school nearly every weekend to see a couple of 40-year-olds and their kids, not even to see anyone my own age.

I signed off with Gert, a quick "next week," leaving her a dollar tip on a dollar snack, and I was out the door. The last piece of road to the school was uphill. Near the leveling-off point, in the rear view were a few of the area's ponds and my favorite open field with one tree set in the middle waiting for lightning to hit it. Then you saw the lawns of Winston ahead.

CHAPTER 4

Winston's entrance was two brick chimney-tall columns with some curlicue bronze on top. You were in a tree tunnel where you could make out a few buildings on either side, and ahead was the student center, classrooms, a dining hall. There was no student center at my school—we sat on the concrete steps of the stadium after lunch. I thought the whole prep school business was comically overrated. Boarding school did not allow for the possibility of being left alone, and was therefore flawed. There was always a concerned teacher, classmate or roommate in your face, from what I could tell.

I remembered the first dinner when I met the Keans. I was visiting my friend Trent who had transferred from Bergenville High to Winston, sent north to get into college despite his C's. I had driven up with his parents who were taking their son's favorite German teacher and his wife out to dinner at the one place in town that had an extra fork at the table. There were heavy velvet drapes and Doric columns between the windows to give the restaurant a Roman atmosphere. I knew Trent from nursery school and our friendship was mostly historical, even at age 15. I'd lost interest in him when he became a late-sleeping, dreamy kid with bitten-down nails and an interest in reptiles. I came to visit him at Winston only to get away from my mother who was already deep into desperate man-seeking and I ended up at dinner with the Keans.

"I hear you're a math whiz and a basketball whiz," was the first thing Shep said to me. He was seated to my left in a coat with elbow patches and a tie.

That he could be impressed with a fifteen-year-old's credentials seemed pathetic.

"Probability plays a large part in life. I'm lucky, I guess." I remember saying that because I had just become interested in combinatorials.

He said, "It took me twelve years to finish my doctoral thesis."

I nodded like I knew what a doctoral thesis was.

"The etymology of German roots from the Middle Ages."

I was sure I had the wrong fork and kept switching from one to the other.

"They don't offer german in my school," I told him.

"You should transfer here," he said, proudly.

I sat back, gave up on the skinny greens and wondered if he was for real. His head floated slightly, and behind his glasses his eyes looked intense and bugged-out. He had taken a liking to Trent which I considered a sign of poor judgment. Trent was an underdog at Winston, a late transfer, an alien with curly hair and a white boy's afro pick, and Mr. Kean clearly identified with him in some martyr's way.

I checked out his wife over the silk flowers. She seemed quietly out of it, calm against his enthusiasm. She seemed peaceful, or totally uninterested in our dinner.

During the meal I could see that she was listening to the grisly details of my home life which Mr. Kean asked about and I was only too glad to add up for him. On the way out, she came up to me and said, "Why don't you visit us again sometime?" I was about the same height as she was in her heels and she smelled like she slept in heavy blankets. Her brown hair was almost right, but unfinished. She had a soft-looking face, a perfectly round face, dark eyes, and deep lines from her nose to the corners of her mouth. Her lips had tiny cracks along the edges and I could see through the lipstick. I looked at her and said, "All right," and when I slept in Trent's dusty dorm room that night before my trip home with his parents, I thought of how I could get back to see the Keans without seeing Trent.

That first dinner, nine months before, seemed long ago and I parked just past the student center at Terri and Shep's dorm, a two-story building across from a little cemetery set in oaks that had low, tipping gravestones. They had the end apartment. Terri and Shep were houseparents at Winston. The apartment was thrown in on top of his teaching salary because the two of them looked after the students living in the dorm. I always held my breath as I parked in front of their building. I had picked up my mother's superstition of

31

doing this every time I passed a cemetery. She believed that if you breathed, you put yourself at some undisclosed risk. When I was younger, I also crossed my second and third fingers on both hands for extra protection.

I checked my watch, 9 A.M., and when I got out of the car, I exhaled. I grabbed my bag from the trunk. It felt airy. I packed very little besides underwear. Sometimes I brought a gift each for Terri and Shep, a book about women for her, some German plays for him, or just candy for the kids, but more often I came empty-handed. The downstairs entrance was crammed with sleds and bats, inflatable swimming rings for little arms, and sneakers, grass-stained into novel colors. Upstairs, the Keans' door had a key in a lock that rang if you turned it and a picture by Gina in crayon that said TRee. I knocked softly once and went in.

My New Jersey home had carpeted floors, but the Keans' were wood, cool on bare feet in the summer, but cold in winter, floors made for sliding in socks. I went left into the living room where I slept, threw my bag on the couch and said, "Hello?" No answer. The curtains in the room lifted like skirts and out the windows long fairways of green headed downhill toward the lake. I was looking out the windows when behind me I heard "Boo!" and it was two of the kids scaring me into a fake jump. Kenny ran at me and threw his 11-year-old 79 pounds against my middle. I hit the wall, slid down it to the floor and Gina slammed against my head with her belly. She yelled again, "Boo!" right to my nose. I got the two of them in a wrestling move and Kenny was already hitting me a little too hard, like I must have hit bigger kids at his age.

I had no brothers or sisters, so these kids were as good as any.

"You go to Clare's concert," Gina said.

"I am?"

"We have to, so you have to," Kenny said.

"Do not," I said.

"Do so," he said, and leaned the ball of his hand on my bottom ribs.

"Anyway, I love Clare's concerts," I said, looking for more trouble although I'm not sure why, seeing I was already on the bottom, the two of them crawling on me.

"They suck," Kenny told me.

"Suck," Gina imitated.

"Clare is a wonderful musician," I told them.

"Clare is a shit," Kenny said. Which was also true.

When I had called the Keans three weeks after meeting them, getting their number from information rather than contacting Trent, I wasn't sure why I was calling. I wasn't sure about either Shep or Terri then, and as I dialed I thought how strange it was to be calling virtually complete strangers in another state for no better reason than a feeling, a hunch that I'd like to see them again, a middle-aged woman with bangs and bad shoes and a career prep school German teacher. Probably I just needed some weekends away from my mother.

Clare had picked up the phone that first time. Of course I didn't know that they had a Clare. She had never come up in conversation at dinner. I tried to be polite.

"Is this the Kean residence?"

"Would it break your heart if it wasn't," came the tart answer.

I realized that my voice didn't sound old enough to command respect. The girl on the other end of the line clearly had an early teenage-sized attitude problem. I guessed from the way she answered the phone that she lived there, but I didn't know who she took me for.

"Who is this?" I asked.

"Who is this?"

"My name is Will Sterling."

"My name is Clare Kean. . . ." There was a pause. "I thought you were someone else," she said, only mildly apologetic.

"Is Terri there?"

She did not answer me but I heard her call 'Mommy dearest' and then Terri came on the line.

"This is Will Sterling. Remember me?"

"I'm so glad you called," she said. "Are you planning another visit?"

We picked a weekend for my visit and she filled me in on bus schedules. Then I said, "I assume that was your daughter. Who did she think I was?"

"She must have thought that you were one of the boys in her class calling to harass her."

"How old is she?" I asked.

"Not old enough to be embarrassed by the way she talked to you. Thirteen."

The next weekend, I took a bus to Connecticut that smelled of exhaust the whole ride. It dropped me at a drug-store in Canaan, Connecticut that had a little cardboard sign set in the window—TICKETS SOLD HERE—next to a diaper sale announcement. Shep came out of a blue station wagon and took the big vinyl bag I had borrowed from my mother. The driver in blue had had to come down and open up one whole side of the bus to retrieve it. It was Saturday, late afternoon and cold in the 30s, and Shep was wearing blue jeans and a white button-down shirt. I could see the tips of my fingers getting red.

"Aren't you cold?" I asked.

"I don't wear coats if it's over 25 degrees," he said. "Makes the winter seem too long."

When we arrived at the apartment, Trent was there. He had learned some etiquette at this school and he came over and shook my hand. I was disappointed to see him and I avoided his eyes in order to look at his hair. It was different from before, a lot flatter and it had a part, although his old curls still hung around the collar.

"Will," he said, "this is great. You're here. It's great."

I didn't know what to say, but then Terri came in and must have seen my dismay right off.

Shep said, "Trent couldn't believe you were coming back so soon when I told him. So I invited him to dinner."

I was quiet through the meal while Shep and Trent told stories about funny school incidents: the football team's bus running out of gas, the sighting of a UFO that brought every-one out of their dorms each night at 9 PM to watch the skies and listen for airy vibrations until the headmaster admitted it was all a prank. Really unbelievably boring stories. I real-ized how tribal the school was with those same sorry incidents getting told at dinner tables across campus every night.

Trent was so excited to have me around (or maybe it was his cranberry juice cocktail), that he told the Keans about sharing a 3D ring with me as a 4-year-old, and how I hacked at a tree in the nursery school yard, killing it, while he took the blame. Shep loved it all as did Clare, who sat on her chair with one knee up and drank orange juice by the quart rather than eating, wearing boys' loose clothes. I could tell she had a crush on Trent. Clare was tiny. I would have guessed her for about eleven if I hadn't known her age. But she had a big brain (straight A's, Shep told me) which she believed gave her the upper hand whenever Terri wanted something from her. She clearly adored her father, but she looked as if she had somewhere to go when Terri approached. Seeing it from Terri's viewpoint, I almost felt sorry for mothers. Then I quickly remembered my own mother. Terri avoided Clare when she could, served the food, and minded the two little ones who were on their good behavior, stuck to their chairs.

After dinner there was a fire and television with two of the kids (Clare gone to her room), and then Trent left with another brisk handshake and a "Great seeing ya."

Shep monopolized me the next day, keeping me busy collecting firewood and repairing, for some unknown reason, a stone wall on the other side of campus. Every time he left the house for one of these chores he would sniff the air at the door and predict the weather for the next six hours.

I spoke with Terri, during a moment alone, only once before it was time to leave. Something about our mutual love of fireworks. But when it was time to get me to the bus and Shep volunteered, Terri said no, she would drive me.

Children with dead parents must give off a scent that is picked up by other children with dead parents. Terri one of us, and the others I'd met in my life I'd gotten along with too, although in most instances we had nothing in common besides the obvious. It was always boys with dead fathers or girls with their mothers gone. The opposite loss group must have had its own scent. I had a name for us: COD's. Children of the Dead.

In the car, Terri and I moved from fireworks to how she liked electrical storms and high winds. She loved standing outside in the rain. She wasn't a bit afraid of lightning. I told her about how at golf tournaments some poor spectator in jackass pants always seemed to get hit by lightning. She just laughed. Then she asked me how I got interested in chance. I told her how people who are ignorant of math compensate by learning facts like when zero became a number or the history of infinity, but in the end they remained ignorant. How people who truly love statistics ask only "Which equations?" and never "Why math?" How probability was not meant to teach us the world, but only what we could say about it. Terri told me about how when she got mad she considered cutting up all of Shep's blazers but she never had. It was that sort of drive to the bus.

Now, many visits later, I was almost part of the family, the part that gets beaten up, and Kenny and Gina were stomping on me.

"Leave that poor, defenseless man alone," Shep told my tormentors. Shep called me a man to make sure the kids knew I was older, somehow separate, not really a blood relation, although I was a frequent visitor.

"Yeah," I said, pitifully, face in my hands, which gave Kenny one more shot at me, slapping down at my back as he stood up.

I tried to be like a man around Shep. I could tell he didn't have many man friends from the way he got serious with me from the start. I had been a little hesitant with him though. I had wanted to tell Shep right off not to invite Trent anymore for my sake during the visits that followed that first knee-slapping dinner with my old nursery school buddy. But I would have had to explain and it would have made me seem bossy and inconsiderate and so I kept this to myself. I hadn't liked Trent in years and he had become your basic modern prep school product, scrubbed and flattened and posed. A dull, good soldier.

But the Trent problem took care of itself. When I arrived for my second visit to the Keans', I was expecting to see him again at dinner and when he didn't show up I went in to watch Terri cook and ask her the evening's plan. Terri and me were already big friends. I should say that Terri liked to hug, which seemed strange at first, but I came to appreciate it; the fact that Trent was not there made me want to hug her. Shep was not a hugger.

"Shep invited Trent," she said, "But he said he was too busy studying."

"Hallelujah," I said.

Dinner without Trent was spectacular, although his absence bothered Clare. She saw me as an intruder, a disrupter, the reason Trent was not coming over. She could do without me. I knew a lot about females from age 16 on from the books Sara fed me, but Clare was a mystery, and her deepest thoughts were not worth my time, I decided after that second visit.

"Shep," I said, still on the floor, Gina pinching my knee, Kenny leaning on my back, "have you ever tried gambling?"

"Uh-oh, you haven't been bitten, have you?"

I wanted to complete the tease, to tell him to call me Shoeless Joe, but he wouldn't have gotten the allusion. Shep hated professional sports.

"Math whiz bankrupts Belmont Raceway. Headline," I said.

"You're kidding."

"Math whiz leaves new gymnasium to Winston School. How would you like to see that in your school paper?"

"You won that much money?"

Shep took everything seriously. Each weekend that I visited, when he saw an opening he told me about a cartoon in the New Yorker that impressed him; he even took cartoons seriously. He would tell me about his latest drive down to New York City to see a play, or about the parents of one of his students who owned such and such a town house in Manhattan. Shep loved everything about New York because it was a serious place and saw me as a New Yorker because I lived closer to it than he did. He told me about German plays and, worse, he would start speaking German to me. Shep was all quick motions and he was wiry. His students must have thought he was eccentric or that he bathed in electricity.

The truth was, I have always been a chicken about money. Wouldn't bet on the tides. My mother, on the other hand, had the golden touch without knowing an integer from a factorial. I figured there couldn't be two of us in one family. That was what probability told me. I had reason to start gambling though. My allowance was stuck at $15. I suppose you could call the monthly poker game with Billy and the boys gambling, but that was lightweight.

Shep said, "Don't tell Terri. She'll flip."

"Shep, I don't gamble."

"So you're not gambling?"

"Not gambling, Shep. Joke. I didn't win any money at Belmont. I've never even been to Belmont."

Terri would have known from the start by the way my eyebrows moved that it was all fantasy.

"Where is Terri?" I asked.

"Errands, studying, somewhere. I don't know. What are your plans for the day?"

Of course I had no plans. I wanted to walk around the apartment and find everything the same. That was enough for me for one day.

"I hear there is a great concert tonight," I said.

"Rest up. It's late. Starts at seven." He winked at me.

Gina whined, "Daddy, when am I going out?" Shep said right away, turned to me and said, "I gotta run her to a friend's. Then I'm jogging. Kenny's off to a soccer game. Help yourself to lunch and I'll see you later."

Shep packed up Gina like a pro, called the time to Kenny, which sent the little goalie dashing out the door with knee-guards, and he followed, holding Gina on a hip and yelling to me some quote from Dickens about poor kids.

Part of being taken care of at the Keans' was being left alone. At my house, if I was in my room thinking or reading, that is, alone, I was in trouble. My mother walked in and said "What's wrong?" in an accusatory way, like she found a dirty magazine and handcuffs on my dresser. She said it without really waiting for an answer, in case something *was* wrong and she had to sit down and talk about it with me. She said it fast because she knew she couldn't help herself from saying it and she had to get it over with. Deep down, she would probably have been interested in hearing a defeated "Yes, something's wrong" answer to this question if she could have been sure that there would be no blame assigned to her. The only time that she didn't walk in on me was if she had a man visiting. Otherwise, in she'd come, talking about an article in the paper or about a distant cousin who had called, or the fact that we were out of tinfoil. She didn't get it. My room. That day and any time that the students were gone on mid-semester break and I had a whole day to go through their dorm rooms, I did so. I thought of those kids as coming from the broken homes of rich people, abandoned to this school in order to have friends their own age become their new family. It was only a matter of time until they stole something or took drugs in the woods and then they were sent to another prep school, somewhat less desirable, stricter, closer to what was once home.

To kill the afternoon waiting for Clare's concert (she was an eighth grader at Winston), I decided to do some exploring. Down the hall from the Keans, the boys' rooms were shameless and pissed me off; they simply couldn't understand they weren't running the world from this school. They were too ambitious and successful, nothing six minutes at the black door couldn't have cured. I could smell in their rooms the long-distance calls for additional cash. I found blonde hair on the pillows, and closets filled with blue blazers, and ties with little tennis rackets. Every room had the newest computer games, so I flicked on the terminals and did some editing for them. Then I opened dresser drawers looking for bank statements. Each unlocked room was the same: the boys were simpletons, perfect conformists.

The girls' rooms were harder to figure out. I remember Shep telling me a story from their first year as houseparents seven years before. A girl had knocked on their door one evening in October holding a note she had found on her door. The note said: "You look like my old girlfriend. Too bad I killed her." The girl was sobbing, and the next day her parents came to move her out of The Winston School. Shep told the story getting angry all over again, still wanting to find the person who had written the note, who by now was long gone, probably out of college and out of medical school, practicing as a psychiatrist. Anyway, the girls' rooms had family pictures on the desks and school newspaper clippings in the corners and good action sports posters, mostly tennis and basketball, the ugly slow white guys from the NBA on the ceiling. There were sneakers and field hockey sticks and school books. I was hesitant to go through the drawers, thinking about Sara.

Terri caught me coming out of a girl's room down the hall from their apartment and I was embarrassed but ignored it. "It's like counting on your fingers when you're a grownup. It's okay to do occasionally, but don't get caught at it too often," she said.

"I was reading this article about men in America, and since I am a man in America I took an interest," I began. We always started mid-conversation. "It said that 51% of births are boys," I told her. "Look at all we have against us. We have a greater likelihood of getting childhood diseases. If we survive childhood, there's a good chance we'll die in an accident and if we survive all that, someone sends us to war. Plus women now live seven years longer. It's preposterous. Without that two percent head start it would be a catastrophe."

"You learned all that on your tour, did you?"

"You bet."

"How are you love-boy? Come give me a hug."

I galloped over to her. She was soft cushions and itchy sweater wool.

"Just some statistics I've been mulling over."

"Obsessing about, it sounds like."

Here's the thing about Terri: she flirted with me just enough, I could tell what she was thinking, and she was never certain about too much.

"How's school?" she asked.

"How's school with you?"

"Hard."

"Mine's easy."

"You're smart."

"You're out of practice."

Terri was studying the history of religion. She drove across the state three days a week to New Haven. Yale Divinity. She wanted a job. Enough babies, as she put it. Vocation, discipline, back to school.

"That's why I'm practicing this afternoon."

"Meaning you're spending it with me," I said, teasing, because I knew she really was meaning to study.

"No, it's me and my friend the bible in the Winston library this afternoon."

"That leaves me here alone."

"You can do it. I know you can. Or you could drive back to New Jersey and spend the weekend with your mother." Terri, of course, knew about me and my mother and had mostly sympathy for the two of us, despite her own babies and their futures. "We'll have dinner and then we'll drive Clare over to her concert."

"Big evening," I said. But it was fine with me. I might drive into town, check out Happy Dog Grooming or the menu at Hal's that advertises fresh seafood although the town was 250 miles from big water. Or swim at Winston's donated natatorium. Or work out on the well-greased weight machines. Or check out college football on TV.

As we walked back down the hall, I said to Terri, "Well, she hooked one."

"Mom?"

"Mom."

"I guess you like him, as usual."

"I don't have to like him. He's with her."

"So you like him."

"Like a man named Lester?"

"A fine name for a man," she said in that play-along voice.

"Well he doesn't seem as shifty as some of the others at least, and he doesn't wear tasseled shoes. . . . No, I don't like him. But I have the feeling I'll be seeing him around."

"If she likes him, she's lucky. Give the old girl a break."

I looked to Terri for instruction about my mother, but after statements like those I was baffled.

When Terri left for the library, I thought of her and religion. Unlike Shep, she hadn't memorized any long passages from holy books and she wasn't even sure of herself quoting short ones. I could imagine her teaching a class. Not a class about strict religion, but maybe people's small problems. She would talk softly. To a college class or a class here at Winston, she would speak about herself or God, but not much about guilt or sin. She went to church every Sunday; she had credentials. I liked to think of her praying. She would stand still and firm, her mind waiting to be filled. It made me afraid of lying to her.

I napped most of the afternoon on the sofa. I left a drool spot.

While Shep made dinner, I played with Gina. She shouted, "3-1-Go," and tried to jump, but she didn't understand jumping at all and only the top half of her hitched upward. Her feet were stuck. I showed her without success. Terri and Shep conferred agitatedly across the kitchen. They had had one big fight during each of my last visits and I couldn't take too much more, since I went there to relax. So I went in, grabbed some yogurt, wax beans, and cheese off the counter, and said, "Don't worry, I'll feed her," to no one in particular and came back out to the dining room to put Gina in her chair. I heard a pot crash behind me, and the quick whoosh and rattle of the refrigerator getting slammed too hard.

Gina downed the yogurt and ignored the other two white piles on her Sesame Street plate. She tipped one end of the plate up and said, "Mo yogu."

I said, "Mo yogu, what?" hoping for some manners.

She said, "Mo yogu, asshole."

At least she said "asshole" clearly. I didn't take it personally. I figured her for a linebacker in twenty or thirty years anyway. I went back into the kitchen for more, and came out followed by Terri, who seemed a little shaky.

Shep came out next and said, "She's not going to the concert."

I kept quiet.

"Too much goddamn work," he said. I could see him shaking too. He was the one who directed the kids through their day, took them to their activities, fixed dinner. If I didn't by nature side with her, I would have been angry at Terri myself. If Clare were there she would have had a fit.

"I'll go with you," I finally said, sounding chipper. Shep looked at me with thanks and headed back into the kitchen, his head floating. Gina was done, as far as I was concerned, so I pulled her off the booster seat, wiped her hands, and directed her toward some blocks.

The concert sucked and so did the rest of the weekend. Terri and I didn't even take our evening walk, but I drove home with good feelings toward all, anyway. I talked with my father on the way; I often spoke with him when I was driving alone. He and I had had good times in cars, driving without destination, just out on a weekend morning, love adding itself to discovery. He had a perfect sense of direction and we talked and talked, the subject not mattering a bit; the trick was to make words keep going through air. Alone on the Connecticut parkways, I would ask him questions about himself, questions that began, "When did I get my first . . .," or "What did you do when . . .," and decided that it was about time that I got around to asking my mother some of the same questions.

CHAPTER 5

Although I'd known Sara since she arrived at Bergenville High eighteen months ago as a freshman transfer, it all really started with her just three days before I met Mr. Lester Warner. I opened the front door of my house pushing back yet more snow and I saw her through the outer storm door. I nudged it a crack further, smiled, and said, "Who's there?"

She had a package in her hands, a small box with a ribbon, and as I looked down on her, she nudged the door open a little more, leaned in, and kissed me.

It was a kiss where I felt a warmth fill my mouth like I had never felt. It didn't last long and when she pulled back, her right hand extended the box and she said, "Happy birthday." I didn't invite her in but I smiled again, this time feeling my face widen and my forehead wrinkle. I didn't know what to say. Of course it was not my birthday, which was in August, so the whole visit seemed odd.

She said, "Well, I was just thinking of you, so I got you something." She turned and jumped off the two steps of my porch and hurried out into the snow, clutching her chest against the wind.

When I closed the door, I realized that the warmth I'd felt had been her tongue in my mouth. I tried to make the saliva in my mouth flow and tried to hold it there to recall the feeling. I felt foolish and proud. Then I remembered that I hadn't really kissed back; I hadn't responded quickly enough. I hadn't responded at all. She had to know I'd never kissed like that before, that all I had known were the dry kisses I'd shared with girls I didn't really like at basement parties. She would probably tell Billy what had happened and they would have a good laugh. Why would she ever kiss an inexperienced guy like me again?

Sara lived two blocks away in a brown two-story house with

stained glass over the front door and a slate walk splitting the front grass into two halves. The Glassers' porch had a hammock. Her parents were elementary school teachers who were kind and lenient. I'm sure they didn't have any idea what Sara knew and did. Her 19-year-old sister was an aspiring actress/singer, but she was a little heavy and overeager so her parents spent a lot of time making Carrie feel better after uninspiring recitals.

The first time I ever saw Sara she was wearing clogs. She was the new girl in the third row of Social Science. When she got up to leave after class, I could hear her bare soles slapping against her wooden shoes which drew my eyes to legs that were strong and athletic, then up over her skirt and sweater to where her black hair was held up by a silver comb. I watched all this, as you can imagine, with some excitement. Outside the classroom I said to her back, "Must be hard to sneak around in those things." When she turned I saw dimples, green eyes, and a little space between her top teeth when she smiled. "Not if you take really small steps," she said.

The day after my "birthday visit," I went over to thank Sara for the present. The snow outside was deep by then, a second storm adding to the earlier snow, and I invited Sara out for an evening snow fight. In the dark, I could see inside the nearby houses and above us her parents sitting in their living room, while the borders of her yard were in shadow. We chased around lobbing powder at each other and I saw she had a good arm, getting me once in the back of the thigh. I kept running and hiding behind trees until I was panting and I finally took her down by the ankles, burying her in the cold snow. I lay near her and kissed her like I had been too dumb to do at my front door. She kissed back and showed me some tricks with her tongue on my teeth while the rhododendron shook over us, our hair got wet, and snow slid into our gloves.

When we went inside, her parents had gone upstairs. We took off our boots and scratched the snow from the cuffs of our pants. She sat at one end of the living room couch and I lay the length of it, putting my head on her lap. My cold finger found a hole on the top of her jeans near her knee, near my cheek, and I pulled it until I could feel my fingertip against her skin. I felt wobbly and nervous and brand-new. I wondered where this hole led to and whether her legs would feel softer if I moved my finger north or south. My palms were itchy and my balls felt like they needed more room in my pants. I was afraid to close my eyes; it would all be over. I knew if they put me in an ambulance, just spatulated me off the couch and put me in an ambulance right then, I would have been diagnosed your basic shock victim. Pale and clammy. It was all too much. Sara did not flinch and she stroked my face. I was afraid to touch her more and was happy with what I had, so I just kept my finger calmly in that hole.

I also knew that Sara had a boyfriend, Gary. He had curly hair and a body that could have been athletic with a little training, strong underneath, but soft, like an old man's body. He was a grade up on me and Sara, owned an eight-year-old Pontiac and probably had sophisticated tastes in music. Before the night that Sara kissed me I might have said hello to Gary without hesitation, although at school we never saw each other, given his English Lit and my math schedules. He and Sara were in some ways similar, from what I could tell—B students, smarter than how they did at school, sexually advanced, occasional class-cutters. But in the end they tried to be good, which I considered a sign of grace in Sara and a sign of weakness in Gary. Sara, for instance, was almost always nice to her parents. Sara and Gary had gotten beyond the rude-to-mom, hang-out-with-Connecticut-adults, not-go-public-with-your-loves stage that I was still in.

After our snowball fight, I went to Sara's house in the evenings to study Spanish and learn about bodies. When my mother was out with Lester Warner I still went to the Glassers', stopping to say hello to them in the kitchen before heading upstairs. We'd lie on the floor of her room on our backs each looking at our books when I inevitably touched her and we began looking at only one book hanging up in the air until I felt my thing getting hard and I had to turn onto my stomach. I'm sure she knew why I did this regular flip but she kept it to herself. Then she would roll over and we'd look at Spanish for a minute or two more until plain rapture began, no questions asked.

I touched everything and she touched everything, but we kept our clothes on for fear her parents, only one room away, would come in and check on us. Life pleased me, not surprisingly. Sometimes I felt my stomach and legs shaking when we went upstairs to study Spanish, just thinking about what was to come. If I had had to explain anything to her about our arrangement, our secret understanding, I would have become gloomy. I knew there was clarity about what was going on between us. We never argued or were aggressive and we found ways not to study much. If, during the evenings I was with her, we went out, we touched secretly. We would brush fingers or bump shoulders, letting go of any longer engagements until we got inside her house. Even her parents were not to know about us; it was too embarrassing. Also, I kept an eye out for Gary's car.

In school, we pretended that nothing had changed between us. She never once asked me why I didn't want to be her boyfriend publicly, why we were sneaking around. This made her the perfect companion because I had no answer to the sneakiness question except that it seemed easier that way. On weekends, I went away and she saw Gary, and when I came home on Sunday night I talked about my time with the Keans. I believe she was impressed that I had such an interest in adults and they had such an interest in me.

Sara said to me one Sunday night, "I think you'll marry young." I knew she thought this was a great compliment. I found it completely incomprehensible but, strangely, a relief.

"Take it back," I said.

"Blond, pixie, cowboy boots, pearl earrings."

"Keep going."

"Ambitious. But a math idiot."

"Never," I told her.

I thought my father would have liked Sara. She was straight, not a bit dizzy, sharp and skewering when she needed to be. I remember walking with her to school in the first months after she moved here, when a man whistled at her. At age fifteen, she stopped, turned to him and snapped, "I wish there was a treatment program for meanness so you could get well." Then she walked away as I struggled to catch up. She had long hands and limbs, a lot of black hair when she let it down, and a harpsichord voice. She also knew French. Spanish was just for fun, languages were easy for her. Of course I didn't know what kind of girls my father liked when he was my age. I never asked him about that. I didn't even know who gave him his first kiss.

In early March, a month or so after my birthday visit, it got more complicated. I did not know what was happening. She seemed a little annoyed and I found myself apologizing at the end of every conversation. I said things like, "I'm sorry if I've done something wrong," although I had no idea what I could have done wrong and she offered no specifics. Then, on a Friday, we didn't even make it into the house for our studying. We sat down on her steps, not even in the hammock. She said, "I hate secrets."

"So do I," I said. "Most of them."

"But not the one we're doing, right?" She sounded annoyed again.

"No."

"No, not this one, or no, it doesn't bother you."

I could see where this was heading, getting trapped in words so early on.

"You're embarrassed by me, aren't you?" she said.

"That's crazy."

"That's not crazy. You touch me in my room. You take my shirt off. Your dick is so hard you have to turn over, and you won't go out with me."

Sara's saying this out loud humiliated me, and I coughed out of nervousness. Bones seemed to be flying around in my head, but at least she knew why I turned over.

"Sara, you have a boyfriend. Remember?" I felt like I had to say smart things, but I didn't have anything smart to say.

"If you wanted to be with me, you'd ask me to make a choice, but you don't even ask me."

I appreciated that she didn't use his name. I knew all this was coming. But so soon? I knew that Sara knew more about guys than I did about girls. It had always seemed as if I had no hope of making up this difference, so I accepted it and learned what I could. But here all she'd taught me wasn't helping.

"Come on," I said in a pleading way, and before I knew it

she was inside the house, the door shut tight. I saw the back of her going up the stairs.

Well, that was that, I figured. Before I took two of the four steps off her porch I realized I was going to see her the next day at the Sidelys', and that neither of us could get out of that rendezvous.

So I was on my way home at seven P.M., two hours earlier than I expected. I had my notebook in my hand, and when a cat walked up to me I stuck my toe under its belly and flipped it in the air. It landed on its toes, collapsing onto its ribs. The ladies of the neighborhood were out. Twelve degrees or one hundred and twelve degrees, they were out. Where were the men? Dead. So the ladies were left to a life of utility trucks arriving every hour of the day to fix breakdowns—roofers, gutter cleaners, plumbers, rug men—and 7 P.M. gossip meetings with their neighbors. A street of widows.

They came out after their dinners alone, and stood in front of one or another's house, determined by some intricate widow schedule. They stood talking in a loose circle, their tiny dogs at their feet also talking together in dog-talk. They all wore sweatshirts with little animals stuck on the front, giraffes, cats. They had fingers with so much gold that when they spread them, it looked like the bars of a cage. They called me Mrs. Sterling's boy. I doubt they knew my first name.

They got nearly giddy when I approached them. Two of them were identical twins who no longer looked alike. The pair had married, in better times, another pair of identical twins and lived six houses apart.

"Good evening, ladies," I said.

One said, "Mrs. Sterling's boy, you want to make a buck?"

They underpaid like crazy. I wouldn't work for them unless my mother made me feel bad about refusing. My mother never came out to stand with them though. This ritual was beneath her; she felt that they were old women and she still had her youth.

"What do you got?" Old people, I've found, like it when you're flip.

"Go down into my basement and catch the family of mice

who are ruining my life. Imagine, I can't even do the laundry."

"What else you have?" I asked.

"Take it or leave it."

"Better get a professional," I told her. Then I barked at her dog, setting the whole canine circle into an uproar, and walked away. That ought to have been enough for an evening of conversation. I was in no mood to get bitten by homeless mice.

When I got in at half-past seven, my mother was already home from her social-work job and she hadn't yet left on her habitual Friday night date with Lester Warner. She helped place foster kids for a state agency, but the pitiful stories never seemed to upset her. I had already eaten, but she invited me to sit down with her anyway. I was going to ask her who gave my father his first kiss. She never offered me much about him, but if I asked about that, more than likely I would end up explaining about Sara, because sometimes I really needed someone to talk to.

"I've got work to do," I told her finally.

"On a Friday night? Aren't you usually out with those friends of yours on Fridays?"

I told her I was going out with friends whenever I went to Sara's.

"Not this Friday."

"I'm going out with Mr. Warner tonight. The new Broadway musical, *Ladies Night Out.*"

"My old friend Lester."

"I'll be staying in the city at Hilda's. I'll be back tomorrow."

In the first months after my father died, she had a few dates, and if she expected one to go late, she called up one of her girlfriends who owned a cramped apartment in Manhattan and spent the night with her. They all thought that she was lucky to have any dates, widowed or divorced themselves, and were glad for her to stay over. They got to hear the dirt first. The first time she called me to say she wouldn't be home, I told her that would be fine. I thought that I wouldn't mind her absence; I would have the house to myself.

But soon after she hung up, it also dawned on me that I might never see her again. Her overnights in the city, this desertion, got me thinking about some strange things. She could get killed by a psycho while waiting for a bus, or just as likely, I could get killed by a suburban psycho in the privacy of my own home. Worried about my safety, I locked every lock on both the front and back doors, even using the chain on the front. It was dark, and outside I saw the illusions of faces. Then I thought that someone was watching me from out there. I thought of her laughing with her friends in New York and began to cry. After checking the windows, I pulled down every shade to the sill, I went into the kitchen, and I talked on the phone to everyone that I knew until 11 P.M. Then I went upstairs to watch TV, turning it up loud so I wouldn't hear any mysterious noises on the stairs or in the kitchen. When it was time to go to sleep, I kept the radio going on the table near my bed, but focused my mind on my own heavy, broken breathing.

If she got killed, I wondered who I'd be left with. I didn't know who she had picked as my guardian. Maybe one of my father's uncles who lived far away. Maybe one of her crazy girlfriends who collected saltines, or shopped only in flea markets, or babied her windowboxes, or felt she had a higher purpose in life. My mother had no family to speak of and there seemed to be no good options for me, which made me angry. How could she take those risks for us? I hoped something bad would happen to me. Then how would she feel? She would never be able to forgive herself.

So usually I called her up at her friend's house, just to make sure that she had come in and that she was okay.

CHAPTER 6

I woke up the next morning and went over again what happened with Sara. I knew I was going to see her that day anyway. The Sidelys were going away for the weekend and were leaving their four kids in my care for chauffeuring, cooking, cleaning up after. That meant no visit to the Keans' but $200 in my pocket from the Sidelys. Actually, they were leaving their two boys in my hands and their two girls in Sara's hands. They had chosen me as caretaker because I used to hang around with their oldest son Ben before he left for college. The one time I'd stayed over, the kids had liked me better than getting sent off to relatives for three days. I recommended Sara to them and said that the two of us worked well together. That brought a smile to Mrs. Sidely's face and one angled eyebrow from Mr. Sidely, and they said fine. They had plenty of money.

I got to their place about 1:00. The car was already loaded. They showed me around the refrigerator, picked out the bedroom for me (Sara got their bedroom), gave me emergency phone numbers, and went down to the basement to tell the kids they were leaving. The kids waved from the playroom without stopping their game. The playroom was arranged to allow for aggression without pain, all the walls and the floor padded with gray gym mats. They had friends over; there must have been ten kids hurling their bodies into corners.

I spent the afternoon just outside this war room, figuring out exactly how much I was making each hour, each minute, each second. I sat on the threshold thinking about how Sara (who was arriving late for dinner so she could spend the day with Gary) would arrive and stalk me, eager to jar me into further mistakes. I tried to devise strategies for avoiding her while not having it look that way. The kids smashed around in the strong lights and the room looked smoky from the dust and excitement. When I came up with no good way to avoid Sara, I thought of math.

Math was a nonhuman language of parts, combinations, and relations. Monster numbers were difficult to manipulate, but simple to think about. It's funny that I can't stand automatic windows in cars or television clickers, when I like numbers so much. Younger kids liked computers, each choice opening to a series of other choices, the betwixt and between seeming alive, but not alive. Kids like Kenny Kean, or those Sidely kids, six through twelve, sugar-delirious, who sat at their little terminals feeling the mysterious power and ease of control. But, as I've said, I enjoyed the simple facts of probabilities and numbers, and did not care much for keyboards and yellow monitors.

It seemed probable that Sara would not speak with me except to ask me things like, "Where's the mayonnaise?" or "Where do they keep the dish soap?" I'd learned however that probabilities were not sure things and Sara could surprise me and arrive with good intentions, a no-grudge holder.

The kids were easy, although I didn't know them well. They all wore glasses and had good manners. I agreed to make one pitcher of lemonade, but that was it. I threatened them once with drowning and the afternoon flew by. I sent the little visitors home at six o'clock and the place suddenly seemed quiet.

Sara walked right by me at 6:30 P.M. When I asked how her day was, she said only "Good, thanks." I was making mac-and-cheese plus hotdogs. The kids grabbed the paper plates that the Sidelys had left for meals, asked for what they wanted and got it, and headed into the living room for a TV meal. Sara sat surrounded by girls on her couch, I sat surrounded by boys on my couch and we watched a video movie agreed upon in advance about parents acting like kids for a day while the kids were the parents. Sara and I were like an old married couple, not talking, not a bit of eye contact. When I asked my boys to stop bouncing on the couch, Sara smirked at me. At 8:00, the youngest two, Sara's girls, got into pajamas, brushed their hair and got goodnight readings. My two boys were sentenced to their rooms soon after; we agreed they could stay up until nine. I remembered bargaining with my sitters when I was younger, hoping that we could go out for ice cream or pizza. I used to hope that they would fall asleep before I did so when my parents walked in I could bring them over to my snoring guardian and the three of us could wake him together. I would then ask for a share of the money they were planning to pay for my care. I told the Sidely boys to read books to each other if they wanted to, but to stay in their room. I heard balls slam against the walls, but no heads.

After I left their room, I went into mine at the end of the hall and threw my few clothes from my bag onto a chair. I made a mess of the place, so it began to feel like my room at home. I went into the bathroom and laid my toothbrush next to the sink. I scouted the medicine cabinets and found only some old Alka-Seltzer and rusty razor blades. I felt old and responsible and young and irresponsible at the same time. Neither of the Sidely boys was much good at sports (I heard the crashing of small objects), but I wouldn't have minded joining them.

Feeling that our business was not finished, I went down the hall from my room to where Sara sat in the master bedroom. I remember that she was wearing a wrap-around brown Indian skirt and a blue blouse. She had taught me to call shirts blouses. She never wore much makeup, so I was surprised to see mascara. I liked that about her. Little surprises. Also that she was a flirt and conspirator. The room was open and neat, the bed had four posts and a canopy. Whatever was about to happen I had the feeling she would not rescue me.

I walked over to the bed and handed her a Hershey's kiss, wrapped in its twisted foil. I always kept candy in my pocket, usually hard candy that didn't melt, but this was a special occasion. I learned this trick from a friend's father who would greet everyone with this sweet gesture.

"You can sit down," Sara said.

"I'll sit on the floor, I'll end up there anyway probably," I said. There was too much silence. "Some things aren't that important," I began, but I saw I'd made a mistake. "That doesn't sound good does it?"

"You know nothing about me, do you?"

"That's not true."

"And you don't mind, do you? If I were on the phone, I'd hang up now and keep everything to myself. So why don't you leave."

She sat straight up, turned toward me. I relaxed. Bad news is almost easier than good news sometimes. I knew that she didn't want me to leave or she would have gotten up and started pushing on me. She's like that, physical and fearless.

"I like you. I like you a lot," she said. "I don't want to be friends with you anymore. I don't want to be just friends. I don't want two boyfriends. I want to know what you think of me. What you think of coming to my house. What you think of coming to my house and doing what we do. What do you want?"

I heard the TV faintly. "Dial this number to hear about your future." I smirked. She thought I was laughing at her.

"You are not even listening," she said.

"I am listening."

"I'm not getting shit from you." She screamed at me and I realized it was the first time I had ever heard her scream.

"You're a cynic. A cynic at sixteen," she said.

I felt a sudden panic with that line; this was all too adult for me. I was frozen. My heart was bouncing in my chest. It was startling and disappointing to think that a decision as important as the one she was laying out needed to be made quickly. Something in me made me want to reject her, some supreme carelessness. But also I had this deeper feeling somewhere: we are important and worth protecting. Mostly I was scared by what I took to be her wildness and sureness. I felt weak and inferior. The situation was a tinder-box.

"And your father's not dead," I said at her tears.

She stopped, paralyzed. I realized suddenly that I had played my trump, a trump I never knew I had before. I felt bad doing it, felt bad that I had given something of his away. But I didn't want to lose her and it was less painful to talk about him than us. I could see her body soften. I saw her collarbone come down, the only bone I ever thought looked like a bone, and I saw the small pocket above it that I loved so much relax.

In the silence, I remembered once wearing a tie of my father's into fifth grade as a joke, and then losing the tie. That evening, my eyes burning, I had to tell him that I lost it. I remember that he questioned me and at the same time stroked my hair. At the end of his questions he asked me to buy him another.

"You never talk about your father," she said.

I shrugged. "It's not worth it."

The room was almost dark, except for TV light. The rest of the house was quiet. No children poked open the door complaining about nightmares or noises. I was nervous and sad at the same time. I had not calculated when I spoke of my father the effect it would have on my voice.

"Go on," she said softly. Sara had a sweet face, just freckles and a few blond hairs on her upper lip.

"I can see my father perfectly clearly," I began. "I remember him just as he stood in the photo in my room. I remember the color of his car and the smell of the peanuts he hid under the seat there. I remember the manila envelope he packed his lunch in. I remember what he cooked for dinner and how much he liked little kids, and the roughness of his fingertips, and the hair on the inside of his forearm."

She must have sat for thirty minutes listening to me. I felt a luxury talking about it, a kind of pleasure. I left out everything about my mother, even when she passed into my head. When I was done Sara leaned over and kissed me softly on the lips. I knew this was why I had spoken of my father, as an aphrodisiac. I had a great longing to strip myself and her, and to roll with her under the canopy, but as she was looking at me with great love for this disclosure, I felt flawed and selfish. She wanted to rest next to me, to lie close to me, so we did until I went to my room.

I lay on my bed, aching and jumpy, listening for any tiny noise that meant she was coming to join me. I thought of her best, naked parts within hand's reach.

I was exhausted and felt pitiful, but I couldn't sleep. I blamed it on the bed, blamed it on the buttons of my shirt which dug into me when I turned onto my stomach, but Sara was all I wanted. The wind kept batting a shutter on the first floor. I heard everything, but no Sara. Hours passed, green numerals separated by a colon, blinking on the clock four inches from my face until I slapped it to the floor, feeling brave sometime near 4 A.M.

At breakfast, my clothes were droopy. She must have sensed that I was upset, but she probably, mistakenly, thought it was about my father. She practically tiptoed around me the rest of the weekend, even dumped the garbage herself.

On Sunday, on my way home with $200 in my pocket, I thought of traffic patterns, statistics theory, and Sara. When a network of streets is already jammed, adding a new street to solve the problem sometimes makes it worse. Traffic moves even slower as drivers pile into the new route, clogging both it and the streets that provide access to it. Sara was a new street to me, easy to find, but causing a lot of congestion.

I was upset by desire, ready to nibble on her and fool around like a maniac. I would have liked to play it differently. When would I be presented again with Sara listening hard to me and feeling benevolent? I should have been candid, calm, and then jumped her bones. It was a big mistake, a critical one, a hollering, aggravated, careless, chickenhearted mistake to be so indecisive when she asked, "What do *you* want?" I felt childish.

As I drove, I kept biting the inside of my cheek and taking shortcuts to avoid stoplights.

CHAPTER 7

Lester, Lester, Lester. I had the urge to tell Terri everything I knew about him after he'd been around about six weeks, but I didn't know much. He was coming around for dinner some evenings, arriving earlier and earlier, but always disappearing before ten P.M. He would be sitting on our couch watching the nightly news on our TV while he leafed through his mail, magazines, bills. I noticed early on that he got postcards from across the country. They had Lester's name on the front and a chess move on the back, along with a rubber-stamped address of the sender. He was a fanatic mail chess opponent, running fifteen games at once, dashing off cards to Kentucky, Wyoming, even Alaska. He kept a magnetic board in his briefcase, a textbook of openings, and a folder of his ongoing games. He offered to play with me, but I refused. How could I win—the possible outcomes were me beating him and putting him in a bad mood or (more likely) him beating me, putting me in a bad mood. I'd seen his face when a man from Miami picked up a pawn on him, or a woman from Topeka put him in check. He fumed. My mother thought that the postcards were ridiculous. He knew enough never to let her touch them; they would have mysteriously disappeared. "Oh, I thought they were garbage." When I yelled at her once for moving my things (I yelled with him sitting right there, listening to Tom Brokaw and moving his knight off to Detroit), he acted as if we weren't in the room. I wanted him to get involved, to defend her, to attack me perhaps, like some of her others had, but he never did. I wanted to tell this to Terri, but when I arrived one Saturday morning and she said that she could not convince anyone else to go horseback riding with her and that I had been elected, I panicked and my mind went black. "Oh no, not me," I said. Kenny had a hockey game and had his pads on at breakfast, Clare and a friend were going into town to a morning lecture on butterflies at the Grover library, to be followed by the hunt itself, and Shep had Gina for the morning by default.

Terri had met the owner of a horse stable in the saddle shop in Lakebury, the horsey little town just north of the campus. I sometimes drove up there and then back to Winston if I arrived too early on a Saturday morning visit and did not want to stop at the Waldorf. The front door of the Lakebury church was bright red and the library was made of oversized sandstone blocks and looked like a fortress. The houses were from the 1750s and had tiny windows. Terri had already made plans when I walked in on the breakfast scene at 8:10 A.M. She said that she had wandered into the saddle shop purely to snoop, but ended up talking to a woman who ran a riding school about reins and oils. Terri had ridden as a girl. I laughed when she said that she learned at the racetrack when her father was not around.

I had never ridden a horse. Horses seemed too big and too smart. They could take care of themselves. The few times I had been close to them they looked gentle enough, but that wet-eyed stare was meant to fool me, I knew, and this deception in the end would mean injury if I got closer. Terri told me to wear jeans and gave me an old pair of Shep's boots along with extra socks. She dug out some old leather boots for herself and said it was a lovely day for a ride in the country. I answered, "If I survive." It was forty-two degrees, a windy March day, and I needed a scarf and hat.

Driving there, Terri said, "Just listen to what they tell you and stay calm."

"What if the horse throws me?"

"Riding school horses are not wild."

I said, "You know the expression, 'If you fall off a horse, get right back home,' well, that's my plan."

I was thinking about the electric steed outside the supermarket that I sometimes put Gina on for a grinding thrill, as we parked outside the corral, or whatever it was called. Mrs. Dickinson came out from the adjoining stable to meet us. She was tall, straight-backed like she was already on a horse, and gray-haired with a red bandanna around her neck. She wore stretchy pants and black boots. Terri did the introductions. I felt ridiculous, but I decided to be brave.

I stuck my hand out to our host. "Give me the fiercest animal," I said.

"I understand you have never ridden," Mrs. D. said simply. "So what we have planned is for one of our trail guides to lead you both through a short course of woods until the young man sees if he likes the experience if that is acceptable to you, Terri dear." Mrs. D. took the horse business seriously.

She opened a small gate into the corral and we followed her onto ground that was soft and turdy. A young woman dressed exactly like Mrs. D led out two horses. Up close, the animals smelled of soap, urine, pine, and leather depending on which way they turned. They looked huge.

"Ponies for you beginners," Mrs. D. announced. I felt my palms suddenly sweating and the underside of my tongue tingle. I envisioned myself on the ground after the fall: pelvis broken, blood clot forming, elbow pointing in the wrong direction.

"I hope someone is planning to teach me how to aim these things," I said, pointing at the beasts.

Our host ignored me. Terri gave me a grimace.

"You do recall how to get on?" Mrs. Dickinson asked Terri.

"I think so," Terri said, and she put one foot into a stirrup, took a hop, and tried to throw her free leg over to the other side of her horse. But she didn't have enough momentum and stumbled, and I caught her falling back, the two of us off balance.

It was a complicated moment. There she was with her back against my chest and I was holding her up, her underarms caught on my forearms, my hands across her chest. I was afraid that she would realize that I was not letting her go, that I was enjoying her softness against me, and I felt my face flush. Then she stepped forward again, collected herself, put her foot back up and made it onto the saddle and the moment was gone. She never looked at me and I relaxed. The rest of the day was fine.

I followed Terri's procedure, but when I was aloft I couldn't believe how far from the ground I was.

"Hold onto the horn and guide with your knees," was the instruction Mrs. Dickinson gave me.

"That's it?" I asked. Mrs Dickinson nodded.

"Sadist," I whispered to myself.

Our horses were linked by the bits (I called them mouth-pieces until Terri corrected me) and our guide led us across the corral to a cut in the electric fence that opened into woods. With every dip I was sure I would slip off and get trampled. I would be dragged back like an extra in a bad Western and no one would notice because my "pony" was last.

We rode for about ten minutes with Terri asking every fifty yards of so if I was all right. My butt bounced gently; math and basketball seemed insignificant as I concentrated on the clopping of my horse's shoes, watching his feet so I could jump when he stumbled. When I was calm enough to look up, it was me and Terri on a skinny trail through white birch, the trees responding to the wind. Out here, I was all hers.

Then, as if we were sitting in her living room, Terri began talking to me about Clare. She looked back over her shoulder when she spoke. I was keeping my attention on my grasping hands and knees. "Terri," I called forward, "my mind is gone."

"No it's not," she said. "You just need something to think about. So help me."

Terri wanted to complain about Clare. The trouble was, Clare had a mean streak. She never thought about anyone's feelings except her own and her father's. She was too close to her father. The trouble was Clare.

"I don't know anything about her," I managed. "She doesn't talk to me."

Our silent guide had turned us in a gentle arc back toward camp. She was obviously bored and planned on keeping the ride under ten minutes. When we returned I would tell Mrs. Dickinson I was ready for a real ride, maybe bareback.

"Exactly. Now why doesn't she?" Terri asked, not picking up that I had no interest in her subject.

"She's always studying," I said.

"Always with the door closed. And she won't let me in."

"She likes books. Terri, isn't that a mother's dream?"

"My dream is for her to have normal relations with people."

"She has friends, doesn't she?" I asked.

"Normal relations with me," Terri said.

I paused. "I don't think that's possible."

"You don't, huh."

"No, I don't. I mean for parents and children in general." I was trying not to be cruel. "My mother and I don't exactly bring out the best in each other."

"You and your mother have real differences."

"You could say that."

"Your mother hasn't exactly been careful with you," she said.

"You could say that."

I was beginning to enjoy this.

"You are a softie, really," Terri said, "and Clare is a tough one."

I wondered if Billy or Sara thought I was a softie, whatever that was. I didn't think my mother would agree with this assessment.

"Clare doesn't talk to you because you're so often here to visit me, and she doesn't want me to have that pleasure."

I had never considered this before. Also I had never heard Terri speak so bluntly about the pleasure of my visits. Yet this difficulty, that somehow my visits took Terri away from her daughter, and that Terri wanted her daughter to change in spite of my visits bothered me a little.

"Clare's okay," was all I said, but I didn't understand about Clare and Terri any better than I understood about my mother and me. About a hundred yards from the corral, I began to wonder who my mother complained to about me, whether she was sarcastic or made excuses for me, or if she considered me a lost cause or a monster. There were only a few times when I had been out-and-out mean to her in pub-lic—when I said to her, in front of one of her dates, that she should color her hair, or when I imitated her style of false laughter. Mostly, however, I stayed away, like Clare did.

What did you do if you were a parent whose child was trouble? I supposed that's what Terri wanted tips on, but I had no conception. I had enough problems as a son. Although I wanted to help Terri, I didn't want to think of her as a mother who needed help.

I said, "Terri, your kids are nearly perfect. Don't worry," and left it at that.

My horse's name was Rex and I gave him a carrot when we got back. I took one for myself so that my mouth would be full and I wouldn't have to talk on our drive back to Winston.

CHAPTER 8

When my mother started serious dating it meant that I did not see her much during the week or on weekends. During the week, my mother stayed at her friends' apartments. She would call our house around five. She would say, "Things are real busy here." That was her code. I would say, "They're real busy here." She'd say, "What would you think if I stayed over at Jean's tonight?" Sometimes I would say, "If you can stand her"; sometimes, "Don't stay up too late." I never suggested I would prefer her at home. Weekends had none of the family obligations she had once imposed to establish normalcy after my father died. The shitty day trips to museums, the visits to farms in order to see real chickens ended after my mother found a few men. I was to fill my own calendar.

At first, I was intrigued in a complaining, troubled way by the thought of my mother meeting new men. Most of her girlfriends had been on that gambit for years, all her widows and divorcees. Billy's mother was content to stay home, he said, with the motto "Once is enough," but my mother had a different idea and all her old friends, women whom she had seen with their husbands over the years until those husbands disappeared too, went out dating like my mother when their turns came. I used to listen to this group of women sitting around in our living room on the odd Friday or Saturday when not one of them had turned up a date with a respectable man, telling funny date stories. They would spread out, one on the mustard sofa, one on the ladder-back chair, one on the floor. No one ever took the loveseat. Pam, who was a guidance counselor and who hid her weight with scarves and vests, used to tell one about going out on a first date with a man she thought was okay, a lawyer, a widower.

"So the guy starts telling me about his big new job, corporate bond sales or something, when I see this piece of paper fluttering down onto the table from his breast pocket. And I see it's his paycheck."

"He just happens to keep his paycheck in his breast pocket. Uh-huh," Linda said. She always got the most indignant about these stories, completely missing the humor in them.

"This paycheck somehow just lands on my butter knife," Pam told her.

"What were you eating?" I wanted to know, which was the most interesting part to me. The men always turned out to be assholes in these stories, so there were no surprises. Plus I felt bad for the men, left to the mercy of those women.

"Pasta," Pam told me. "Does it matter?"

"Of course it landed numbers side up," my mother added.

"Just so happened," Pam said. We all wanted to know his salary but Pam said she was so disgusted by the whole incident, and embarrassed and surprised, she didn't bother to look.

Then Sherry told one about a romantic date—dinner, a movie.

"I brought him back to my building and I had some groceries in the car. He tells me not to bother with the food, he'll get it. We nearly get into a fight over this. I let him into my car trunk and go upstairs to open the apartment. I get upstairs, but he never arrived. I go down to look for him and he's disappeared."

Linda said, "Scum," and the rest of the group nodded in agreement.

"Men have no patience," Renata said. "I once went out with a man who loved music. He took me to concerts and operas even to listen to visiting orchestras. His house was filled with complex musical appliances. I was afraid to touch any of them. But he used to cancel half the dates he planned with me."

"He had another girlfriend, right?" my mother asked.

"Worse. He used to try to upgrade his stereo system all the time. So if there was a sale on a Saturday, he would call me at the last minute and say he had to run somewhere to pick up a new speaker or gadget."

Once I told the group about the woman who met a man in the elevator of her apartment building.

"'I haven't seen you here before," she said to him. "Have you lived here long?" She was excited by her luck.

"I've been gone thirty years," he told her.

"Where have you been?" she asked.

"In jail. I murdered my wife and chopped her into little pieces with a hatchet and buried her in garbage bags."

"Oh, so you're single," she answered."

They all sort of chuckled at this one and wondered where I had heard such a joke. In the end, they probably thought I knew nothing about their problems.

These women, probably smart women before they lost their minds, had become believers in fate and mystery, and I couldn't stand believers in mystery. They were self-deceivers, runners from facts, make-over artists. People who couldn't and didn't want to explain a thing about themselves in any truthful way. One of them had the nerve to say to me, "Love is an emotion that I have no interest in finding out about again."

Which of course was garbage.

This affected me deeply though, because it was my mother who said it, and said it at a time when my interest in Sara was on the rise toward love.

Dating nights for my mother were empty-house nights for me and empty-house night meant parties. I would call Billy and ask him over to talk about Sara. Billy would go off about sex, and condoms not fitting him, and tell the one about the microscope and tweezer. I'd have the table set for the perfect meal. I would make one green, one red and one white food for dinner. Billy would sit back and let me cook like he was expecting it. The few times his mother was out and we were at his house we'd order pizza. At my house, I wore an apron, and we would eat like adults and talk about sex. Billy would tell the one about the big G. "Three black ladies sitting around in heaven. One turns to the other and says, 'What you die of?' 'The big C,' she says, 'I had cancer.' And the two other ladies say, 'Ahhh.' The second lady says, 'I died of the big H. I had a heart attack.' And the other two say, 'Ahhh.' The third lady says, 'I died of the big G.' 'The big G?' they ask. 'Yeah, I had me gonorrhea.' 'You can't die of gonorrhea,' they say. 'If you give it to Leroy you do.'" Billy had perfect teeth when he laughed, and his little ears inched up.

In my best black voice I'd tell Billy the one about the guy who goes to buy a Cadillac. The dealer asks him, "You thinking of buying a car?" and the man says, "I *know* I'm gonna buy a car, I'm thinking about pussy."

Jokes got Billy talking about Linda, telling me her nipples were like the dials on gym lockers. Which got me thinking about Sara. Billy liked girls with a throw-down quality. Girls like that scared me. I reserved everything I knew about Sara's loveliness and told him everything I desired about her instead. We'd put about two-thirds of the dishes in the sink, then we'd go across the street and shoot around at the elementary school court until it got dark.

Billy was a genius at basketball because it didn't matter to him, not as much as keeping things good for his mother, or sex. Billy preferred happy talk, so it never got too serious. He liked to observe but not scrutinize. Billy imitated news anchors and comedians and gym talk until we wobbled with laughter and sat down on the asphalt. Then we would tell about the latest murder stories we'd read in the paper. We would rip them out and keep them soggy and crumpled in our pockets until we next saw each other. They were like jokes to us, but sick, and we loved it. Murderers saying things like "We had a beef. He had a knife. I had a gun. So I shot him." Sometimes, good murder stories were better than good sex jokes. We especially liked murder stories that involved teachers obsessed with students. Teachers who kept cattle prods and whips in their houses, and who sent anonymous valentines to their favorites year round, until they lost control and the stalking started, leading to the inevitable murder or suicide. We'd shoot around and talk about whether we preferred playing on asphalt or cement or the wood on old gym floors, and what kinds of backboards we shot best at, and who in the NBA had most recently busted a backboard, and then we got into trivia and statistics.

I used to call Sara if Billy wasn't home. She invited me to dinner some nights when she heard that I was alone and once I invited her when my mother was gone. I had the food picked out when she came in and we cooked together, like it was a dinner party except no one was coming but us. I did drinks and desserts. She was better with spices. I reached around her, leaned past, bumped elbows with her; breathlessly, and with difficulty, stayed alive.

I told Billy or Sara, whoever was there, that my mother would be home later, much later. Neither of them ever asked where my mother was exactly and if they had I probably would have lied. I couldn't hear myself saying, "Yeah, she's staying over in New York having fun."

Things were at a low just before Lester came on the scene. Just the month before, my mother had gone crazy. "To find better men," she considered renting her own apartment in New York instead of just staying with her friends.

One evening, I was working at my desk on the blotter my mother kept replacing, occasionally looking out the side window where I could watch the three-legged dog penned up next door, when my mother came in and sat down on the bed across from me. She crossed her legs and said, "I think I'm gonna get my own apartment near work."

My answer was, "You can't afford it." I sat back, crossed fingers behind my hat.

I regularly did all the numbers in her checkbook. When a bank statement came in, I went to work. I knew that checks paying for parking tickets got cashed fast but checks for sewer bills got cashed slowly. I knew what accounts she had outside of checking, where she transferred her money. I didn't know how much she got for my father dying, where it went, at what interest, and this bothered me, but I knew almost everything else about her deposits. She had handed this responsibility over to me after my father died she said to teach me discipline, but really because I could add and she could not.

"I've added it up," she said, "and I can afford it."

I said, "Send me a change of address card," and turned back to my work.

"Don't you want to talk about this?"

"It doesn't seem so, does it?"

"I think you should talk about it."

"Really?"

"I can't do this commute every night during the winter.

You know I'm afraid I'll have an accident, I'll lose control, slide on the ice."

"Hire a driver."

"You can use it when I'm there and when I'm not there. On weekends."

A bribe. How clever of her. That's when I first had the idea to go away every weekend for the rest of my life. Of course it was a Friday night that this conversation was happening.

"It's a cute little place. You'll like it. It has one bedroom, a smallish kitchen. The living room looks out at the river."

So she had actually been shopping around.

"Sounds great. What can I say?"

"You know that this is only for emergencies. Maybe once a month. And on those nights you can stay with a friend. Or I'll leave you money for dinner and you can stay alone."

The whole thing was unbelievable to me, even if it was only once a month. Of course I didn't really want her to be home, I only wanted her to want to be home.

I said, "Well, it sounds great."

"Say you're happy for me."

I couldn't say it. I could feel myself getting tired, wanting to lie down.

I said, "I'm tired. I want to lie down."

She looked at me with her look of 5-minute dismay—she would not consider how I felt again after five minutes had passed.

"Tell me what you'd like me to bring from here to furnish it, what things of yours you might want there." She rose and left without closing the door behind her.

Sometimes, you can't explain why or how, but you're acting and almost believing it's real. That's how I felt when I said I was tired. I wanted to be tired, but I wasn't. I was simply angry in an awful, wall-punching way. I paced around the room bouncing a Ping-Pong ball and found myself speaking with my father. I told him that boys my age usually don't know very much about their mothers, and only maybe, just might take an interest later in them, but look what his leaving had done. My mother had become a desperate woman, a woman on the run. Worse, she expected me to know this and to reassure her that it was okay for her to move out on me.

That week, I began stealing from her. I would take twenty dollars from the soft wallet hidden in her middle drawer under the socks. I would take bills from her bag when she left it hanging on a door knob. At the same time, I became friendly with her again. I picked up some of her housework. I started ironing, and washing a few dishes. I put the money I stole into my account, telling myself it was what my father left for me. Better than her spending it.

Two weeks later, when she told me to forget about a New York apartment (she said it as if I had wanted one), my mother began sending me letters from work. Fifteen-year-olds do not get mail, except sports magazines or a few cards from faraway camp romances if you've been to camp, which stop arriving about November. So when her letters arrived and I saw her sharp blue penstrokes and my name on the envelope, I was surprised and wary. As I ripped into them, I expected lectures, reminders, or apologies, but she would write between one and three words on her stationery, phrases like: "For your interest," or "Read this," and enclose newspaper and magazine clippings. She sent me stories about children living below the poverty line, about the benefits of single-parent households. She sent nothing I would be interested in except one about sexually transmitted diseases. She sent me stuff about health food and why teenage boys don't get scared by horror movies. Of course she didn't know that I had just taken a new interest in these movies. I liked the fear and I was sick of all the other movies with the winners winning, the husband and wife reuniting, the kindly space creatures.

Doing my shopping (I was a coupon expert at 14) with the money she left me on the nights she was gone, would sometimes remind me of her. I was in a bakery buying cinnamon buns and said to the woman behind the counter, "I'd like to buy three cinnamons."

"Which kind, large or small?" She was bending into the case.

"What's the difference between them?" I couldn't see to the back rows.

She stood up. "This is small and this is large," she said,

putting the first finger and thumb of her two hands together into a circle and expanding.

"Okay, three large," I told her.

"We don't have large," she said.

I looked at her and started to laugh wildly. I thought of my mother who was putting me though a similar exercise it seemed.

In those weeks before Lester, she looked strange and spooked and out of place.

I once said, "Home to pick up your mail?" to make her feel bad, but usually I stayed away from her unless she cornered me. She was always nervous, as if something might go wrong at any moment. But it already had gone wrong.

"Oh, thanks for the letters," I said.

"You like them?"

"No." Then I walked away.

CHAPTER 9

Lester was against the idea and so was I, but it didn't matter to my mother. Early in April, for no apparent reason, she advertised for a boarder in our local paper—twenty five dollars per week for twenty five words. I didn't get to help her prepare the ad. There was an extra room next to mine that was used to store junk—old furniture, kindergarten papers, my mother's photo albums—a room whose charm was the fact that it was never cleaned. This was to be the boarder's room and my mother hired someone to buff it up a bit, fix some hinges and windows, put hospital corners on the too-soft single bed.

The three lines in the paper read, "In search of an adult, quiet and responsible to associate with a family of two in a private home. Lovely refurbished room."

When the interviewees began to arrive carrying the ad, I saw it for the first time. Despite the particular wording, my mother merely wanted a boarder who had no weird habits or stunts, to help her pay the mortgage. She also did not want to leave me home alone too many nights. I wanted a slave; I wanted this boarder to cook, vacuum, clean ovens, and drive me where I wanted.

We interviewed a few students who were attending the local community college, one "former" alcoholic who was trying to make his way back, a woman who was thinking of separating from her "lovemate," and a Guatemalan family of four who thought the room was perfect.

Phil Churney had a Midwestern friendliness that my mother seemed to like immediately, but which put me in mind of coroners. Prospective renters usually made right for the advertised room (during their day of visiting dozens of such rooms), but I heard my mother chatting with this one for more than ten minutes before they went upstairs. I was in the room waiting when my mother introduced us and showed him the accommodations.

"This is it," she said, extending her hand into the room. His sweeping view was of a bed with a brown and purple cover, a chest with a swiveling mirror, an old door made into a desk and bracketed into a corner with a file cabinet underneath for extra support. There was a picture of a cowboy on a bucking horse that I had contributed from the back of my closet.

He smiled. "I love antiques," he said.

He had brown bangs, gray eyes, big perfect teeth, and his clothes were a little baggy. He also had a well-groomed mustache that went just past the corners of his mouth. I figured him for twice my age.

"Leftovers," I said.

He went inside to get closer to the horse and rider. There was enough room to walk four paces from the bed to the door if he was the pacing type. The picture was at three paces.

"I'll take it," he said.

"The price," my mother said, "we'll have to discuss separately."

That meant without me.

"The price is $185 a month," I told him. "Take it or leave it."

"Yessiree," he said, and that was it.

My mother shook his hand but I wouldn't, wanting to set a few groundrules first. No coming into my room when the door was closed, roll the toothpaste from the bottom only, and the driving, cooking, and vacuuming that he would have to understand were now his responsibilities, although he could ask me questions.

He moved in that day.

He was a teacher in a competitor high school and with classes about to begin I didn't have a conversation with him for several days. He left early, came home late.

We met up in the kitchen one night when my mother was not home. She was staying in the city. He had cooked tapioca for himself that looked like fisheyes in milk. He had hard-to-read facial expressions because mostly he smiled, and I did not trust him. His tongue wiped his mustache even when he wasn't eating. He took a gamble with me almost immediately.

"Are you a momma's boy?" he asked as I was getting an apple.

"Hardly," I said.

"You have a girl?"

This was tricky. Sara was new to my imagination.

"Let's say I'm in the training program," I said.

"You mean you're no good at girls," he said.

"I mean I'm not telling you nothing."

"I had a girl at your age," he said.

I gave him my nothing look.

"You believe me?" he asked.

I was quiet.

"I had lust in my knuckles."

"Fascinating," I said.

"What I'm saying is, it'll come." And he licked his mustache.

I accepted his challenge and stopped short of telling him any truths about myself.

School was his work and school was my work so we had something in common. He was stupid enough to give the parents of his worst students his home phone number, our phone number. A parent called each night, returning his daytime call, to give excuses why their child had not been in class that today, to explain that little Sammie or Samantha had lost the latest assignment.

I only wanted from him a few tips as to how to do less in class and get away with it. Also maybe a few about girls.

Within the week he had me grading his biology papers, watching half his class get in the 40s. I knew why our school always beat theirs in basketball—they were morons. I called stupid kids stupid; he called them academically troubled, sounding too much like a guidance counselor for his own good.

My mother was just glad we were getting along. She could stay away more, leaving me with an older male she believed could be my friend and a good influence. But most of my respect for him was gone when he challenged me to a game of basketball. Just watching him go down the stairs flat-footed I could tell he was completely uncoordinated.

"I'll kick your ass," he said. He shot a one-hand-from-the-hip number and headed for the rebound before it left his fingers. He had no accuracy. He tried to body me closer in, backing me up with his bony butt but I was too fast. He played like the math geniuses in my class, running, circling to no purpose. His skin got all pink and I made him sit down and rest. The second game I spotted him points.

"Don't tell my students," he made me swear, "or their parents."

When we got in, he offered me a beer from one of the six-packs he always kept cold in the refrigerator, squeezing my food into the vegetable drawers and corners. While he took big, moustache-frothing chugs, I sipped, appreciating the cold but not liking the taste. I wanted him to think I was casual with my liquor however.

He said, "Take it easy with that. Not all at once." Then he said, speaking of himself, "Cool on the inside, now for cool on the outside," and he went upstairs to take a shower.

Despite his big-jointed, craning body he would walk around the house in his post-shower towel for hours, proud of his skinny muscles. He put on cologne, picked shirts from his closet by the smell of their underarms, and told me everything he knew about girls in an enthusiastic and confident way. He told me that girls liked cars (his favorite was the Jaguar, pronounced "Jagwire," which he was saving his money to buy), and clothes and gentleness. Terri had already informed me about girls liking gentleness.

Churney was as girl-crazy as any kid in my school, but subtle about it. He took me with him once to buy fish for dinner. Inside the shop there was the sound of water running and the requisite nets, lobster traps, rusty hooks, and dried crab claws on the ceiling, as well as a long glass case of waxy-eyed fish corpses. It was like a visit to a toxic seashore. Behind the glass in a hip-boot and apron getup was a young woman with a shiny face and lots of blonde hair pulled back tight. Churney started pacing back and forth along the case searching for the perfect filet. He'd look up at her, shake his head, and stare down again into the case.

I said to him, "Buy a fish, will ya?"

The girl gave me a big grin, but he missed it, his head down.

"Contain yourself," he said. "We have to be particular."

He said "we" but I knew he meant himself and her, the blonde.

He stood up finally and I could tell he was checking her out because she was checking me out.

"Could you hold those two up?" he asked, pointing at two pink triangular filets about the length of telephone receivers.

She slid open her side of the case, fingertipped the two nice ones, then stood and held them vertically, side by side, in front of her chest. They looked wet and the meat opened up a little as they pulled down so you could see through to the silver skin in back.

He said to her, pointing, "What do you think of those?"

"They look good to me," she said.

He shuffled around, staring at the fish flesh like he was buying art; I thought her arms would get tired, but she kept the pieces up. "You look like someone who'd know if they were good," he said. "Wrap 'em up please if you'd be so kind."

She put them in white paper while he took a toothpick off the counter and put it in his mouth.

"Much obliged," he said when he paid.

"Much obliged?" I asked him when we got out. "What was that all about, much obliged?"

He said, "Be particular with your fish." But I knew he meant girls.

"You tortured her," I said.

"Just getting to know her," he said.

It was little adventures like that which made me realize that Churney was closer to me in thought and ambition than he was to my mother or, for that matter to any of the teachers in my school, and it made me think twice about all my favorite teachers. I knew my father would have found Churney as humorous a companion as I did. But if one of my school teachers had been like Churney, my father would have given him only a weary, polite nod and probably not even a handshake.

I came home from Billy's one night around nine and after

making myself an eggcream headed up to my room. At the top of the stairs I saw that his door was open a crack and when I moved towards it I heard little hoots, mock laughter, and sounds of thanks that slowed me down. The crack was about one eye wide so I made the most of it. Churney never called them girls, always mommas, tickets, or governments. "Talk to my government," I had heard him say to friends wanting to see him on a weekend night when he had other plans. Inside his room I heard the voice of the government. I was trying to see around the closed part of the door, wishing that I had one of those dentist mirrors. My one eye and my one-eyed trouser snake were bulging to see the action. On the half-bed that I could make out, there was leg grabbing and hip adjusting. They were undeniably naked and I watched it unfold. Churney looked happy until he got the sense that they weren't alone. I saw the thought pass over his face. He got up slowly, said, "I better shut the door," and came toward me, his thing looking greasy. He was real cool so as not to get her upset and he pushed the door in my face.

I don't think that he was embarrassed for himself. He just didn't want to make this peeping a habit, given the risk to his lovelife if the girl found out.

I was certain that a man-to-man was forthcoming. But when we passed the next day he asked me, "Take any notes?" and that was it.

CHAPTER 10

Churney left two weeks after arriving. He took his own place so that he could have some privacy, I guessed. I wouldn't be there knocking on his closed door when I heard him and someone in there doing it anymore. I had to believe that he knew what he was getting into, moving into our house and taking me on as a protege. It just had not worked out from his standpoint. I felt as if I'd let him down.

The day after Churney left, Lester was visiting and tried to badmouth Churney to me. "How can a person like that be a teacher? Who would hire him?" Lester asked. "If he were my son's teacher, I'd raise hell." Lester was often talking about "raising hell," but I had never witnessed the act. I didn't agree with Lester's opinion of Churney. It was Lester's first loud opinion on a subject that involved our family, and not his own affairs directly. I didn't agree with him and I didn't appreciate his butting in. I whispered to my mother, "It's none of his business," but she wasn't listening to either of us.

I missed Churney's gawky company, his coming out of the bathtub with a shower cap on; I missed his soy hotdogs in the freezer and his cologne stinking up the hallway. I missed his talking on the phone, working the wax out of the opposite ear with a match.

My mother's income-producing bid a surrogate brother for me had failed. She was not very observant and thought we could just get someone else, but I, with my strange loyalty to Churney, set new guidelines that would prevent us from getting a replacement. I told her that there were enough comings and goings with her and her men-friends. I told her that my having a house-mate did not make my life or her life any more certain. I told her she had enough money in the bank without taking on another boarder. She looked gloomy and agreed.

The truth can be made up if you know how.

I told her that all we needed was to take in some closet pill addict who loved his own voice, who had a perfect memory for boring times, telling me about his joint aches and hurts, some old whiner who stole from us. That sealed it.

I saw Churney only once more after he moved out. He called a few times to ask how I was, but we never were able to get together and then he stopped calling. I assumed that he had found a new government, probably a dictator who had made some changes in his home duties.

Billy and I, besides sharing a taste for newspaper murder stories, also enjoyed some action, so on an occasional Friday night we would hang out on the curb across the street from Holy Charity's Emergency room. It was a hospital half the size of Dr. Kuhn's Bergenville General but it had an ambulance entrance right on a side street, and sliding doors with big red crosses on them. We would get there around 8:00 so that it was dark and we wouldn't have to see anything too clearly. We were a little squeamish.

On our first visits, a year or so before, we had expected to see your basic broken legs or breathing troubles, but what we saw was far worse so we kept going back. The whole scene became addictive: the red gyroscope on the ambulance (the AMBULANCE printed reversed and backward on the bumper so that it inverted perfectly in the rearview mirror, which I thought was the invention of a true genius), the nurses coming out to meet the wounded, and the ambulance drivers always calm, never in a hurry. We had our favorites: the hysterical ones strapped down, the neck injuries, the old folks in diapers who no one wanted to touch, the big tattooed man whimpering.

After about six months, Billy found out that a girl in our class worked some night shifts in the ER as a volunteer. At about two years of age she had decided that she would become a doctor and had begun volunteering. She began as a candystriper, but had worked her way up to running blood from the new admits, taking hot blood in tubes up to the lab for tests. She used to let us into the ER. We said we were thinking of being volunteers. I think she had a sweet spot for Billy.

The emergency room itself held about eight stretchers,

each one surrounded only by a high-water curtain. You could see the ankles and feet of nurse, doctor, and blood drawer.

So we got the stories. The 70-year-old man who stood up in his rowboat for a piss and fell into 45-degree water. The lady who, strangely, only had seizures in restaurants and hadn't paid for a meal in years.

The Friday after Churney left, we were sitting as always beside the nursing station on tall metal stools, when I heard, "I got a drip," in a familiar voice behind a curtain.

The nurse said, "Well, let me see."

"I'll just take the antidote and be on my way," the man's voice said.

"After I swab it," she said.

"That won't be necessary."

"We need to know what we're treating," she said.

About ten minutes later, she went in with a needle and syringe and then I saw Churney come out.

He saw me staring. "The wonders of confidentiality," he said.

"Not your day, huh," I said.

"No one to blame but me, sport."

"Hardly seems worth it," I said.

"Just fell out of my pants," he said. "Some day you'll understand."

I tried to imagine how that happened and Billy had some ideas too after I told him that Churney wore only Jockeys without the convenient opening. He told me that some people just lose things easily.

"They're called losers," he said. I had a more conventional view of Churney's heroics, but Billy and I could not agree on a definitive version.

CHAPTER 11

At the end of April, I drove to the Keans' on Friday after a math exam, arriving at Winston around 6 P.M. Kenny, with his lacrosse stick, was hurling balls against the brick of his building as I started inside.

"Tell them to hurry up," he said. "I'm hungry."

"All famous athletes are hungry," I said.

He answered, "Yeah," but I'm sure he didn't get it.

I went up the stairs and into the apartment. I threw my bag down, noticed that Clare's door was closed as usual—she was probably studying—and I heard Gina just getting out of her bath.

Shep came out of the kitchen and said, "Just in time for some fine dining hall cuisine. How was the drive?"

The truth was I'd gotten stuck behind a tiny women with curlers and driving a Chrysler on the final two-lane stretch into Grover. I must have leaned on my horn for about three miles without effect. I watched the unmoving curlers: she never checked her mirrors. "Your typical leisurely country drive," I said.

Terri came out of the bathroom, the pants over her knees wet with bath water. She waved and said, "Gina's learning about tidal waves."

"Blow bubbles," Gina said and ran nude into her room. Her butt was dimpled and red.

It took about thirty-five minutes to get out of the apartment. While waiting, I read the sports section of the Berkshire Squire. The paper included only two columns of pro sports and about six pages of local girls' volleyball and swimming results. There was a commentary about ice fishing. Around me, there were the familiar negotiations about getting dressed, a discussion of how cold it was outside, and then the exaggerated screaming and the running toward the door when Terri said, "Well let's not miss dinner."

We walked the two hundred yards to the main building in the dark. My breath came out gray in the cold air. Shep led the way, Clare at his side. Students were heading back to their dorms, girls chasing boys, hearty shouts echoing through the trees. Ivy grew from the dorms we passed like on the best houses in Bergenville.

Inside, the main building was cool and quiet with a ceramic floor of hexameters, which I knew from math fit infinitely. Huge arched windows across from the entry opened during daylight onto an expanse of green. They were just black at night. It was like looking into an empty mouth. From previous explorations I knew that the hallways to the left and right of the entrance led to classrooms where the rich kids sat in coats, ties, and loafers, in perfect class sizes, looking attentive, but waiting to get back to their grownup-free dorms to set fires or smash mirrors. The dining hall was in the basement.

When we got downstairs most of it was empty already. The kitchen closed in fifteen minutes, at 7 P.M. A few kids in turtlenecks sat at round wooden tables pushing food around with their forks and fingers, lingering. I felt superior to them because I had come to eat with a family and they were alone with each other. There were two openings—one in, one out—leading back to the kitchen where you pushed a tray along and got served by townies earning a few bucks cooking and cleaning up after the Winston kids. The workers moved apathetically in their white net hats. We were the only ones on line. I took Swiss steak, rice, broccoli, and chocolate pudding. Kenny took Swiss steak and four puddings, Clare just rice, and Terri and Shep had salads. They brought an extra plate for Gina who ate bits of everyone else's dinner.

On the way to our table, Terri said to Clare, "Just rice again?"

"If they made it red or blue it would be more interesting," Clare said.

"She'll have fruit too. It's okay," Shep said.

Terri said, "Rice and fruit is not a dinner," and left it at that.

We all sat at a round table off to the side of the in-door, Gina on a booster seat Shep had dragged over from the corner. There was the basic conversation about what each of us had done that day. Terri had been to New Haven for classes, Shep had taught German 1 and 2 and been to a faculty meeting which Kenny called a "faulty" meeting. Kenny kept interrupting everyone's stories, telling us what a jerk this or that one of his classmates was. I talked about math class. Clare was silent, pressing a few grains of rice between her fork tines and passing it into her mouth. She was very skinny, but with her gray eyes and slim lips, she looked like Terri.

There was a chair-scraping commotion across the room that we turned toward only when a tray crashed over and a glass rolled to a halt. One of the older boys was stumbling from table to table headed toward the kitchen.

Clare looked up and said, "Not again."

Shep mumbled, "How many times . . . ," and pushed his chair out.

"It's always the PGs," Terri informed me. I knew that stood for Post-Graduates, a prep term for taking an extra year of high school before applying to college. In my school they called it "left back," but here the arrangement was used by the school to enhance a weak football squad and explore the "college potential" of the PG.

"Hey Christopher, are you having some trouble there?" Shep called out.

"No, I'm not, Mr. Kean," beefy, thick-thighed Chris called back. "Not a bit Mr. Kean." He stumbled toward our table near the in-door.

"I'd say you were," Shep said.

"I'm just weak from not eating after practice."

Mr. PG was obviously a complete idiot, drunk up to his bloodshot eyes. Kenny and Clare were giving him impatient stares.

"What's in the bag in your hand?" Kenny asked.

"Kenny Kean, you keep quiet," Terri told him.

Crafty old Christopher tried to hide the paper bag behind his beefy leg. He was about ten feet from our table.

Shep stood up. "Give me the bag," he said, moving toward the wobbling student.

"I don't think you need it," Chris said. "It's an empty bag."

"He means, an empty bottle," I whispered to Terri.

"I think if you don't give it to me now you won't be in this school much longer."

"Mr. Kean, I'm just going to get dinner. Is that okay?"

I knew Shep was going to be hard on him, for Chris's sake, for the school's sake, and not least, for our sake. Chris was about twice the width of Shep when they stood side by side.

"This is embarrassing Chris. Give me that bottle and get out of here," Shep said. "I'm not going to even ask where you got it if you give it to me now. We can talk about all this tomorrow."

Chris was still denying that there was a problem.

"A guy can drink Gatorade, can't he? Can't he, Mr. Kean?"

"Am I going to have to take that bottle from you?" Shep said tightly.

"Not my Gatorade," Chris answered, hugging the bag to his chest. The few other students in the dining hall giggled.

"Take it Dad," Kenny screamed. Gina was clapping.

Terri was moving now. When she reached Shep and Chris, I saw she had a tray in her hand with two of Jerry's puddings on it. "Take these puddings to your room, eat them and go to sleep," she said, guiding Chris's back with her hand toward the exit. He still had the paper bag.

Shep made one last try. "Give me the bag," he yelled.

"It really doesn't matter," Terri said.

Everyone watched as she led him out the door. Then the other students got up and left too. Terri came back in a few minutes. We were all at the table, alone in the room, faking like we were eating.

"Dad, you should have . . . ," Kenny started.

"That's enough," Terri said.

Then Shep gave Kenny and Clare a speech about manners, proper behavior, and alcohol. He knew he had been shown up for trying too hard and I knew his argument with Terri would be resumed later. Arguments always were.

When we got back to the apartment, Terri put Gina into pajamas, carried her to bed, and assigned the others to clean up their rooms until bedtime. Clare's room was always neat, but she was glad to go to her books nonetheless. Terri then came into the living room to watch TV with me while Shep stayed in their bedroom. Terri was distracted and lasted through maybe fifteen minutes of a National Geographic special about the mating patterns of rain forest birds before she said good night.

When I brushed my teeth at eleven, she and Shep were still at it behind their door.

I heard Shep get up and leave on his morning run. Through the window the sky was purple behind a slash of high clouds and I shut my eyes again. When Shep next woke me, I knew from the smells and noise that it was late. Everything sounded a little too loud.

"Why are you still sleeping?" he asked me, sitting down on the far end of the bed in his running clothes. It was then that I realized that swallowing was extremely painful.

"I think I'm sick," I announced, not quite sure.

"Do you know why?" Shep asked.

This seemed like a strange question, and I was just becoming aware of my headache, so I said, "No, I guess I'm just sick." I remembered the drunk boy in the cafeteria from the night before and I was suddenly certain that he felt fine this morning while I felt hungover.

"Yes, of course," Shep said, "but what's wrong with you?"

"I don't know."

"Which part is bad?"

"Shep, I think I'm going to die, okay?" I was ready to doze off again, ready for him to leave me alone.

"That's silly," he said.

"Everyone who's sick thinks they're going to die," I mumbled, burying my head.

Shep hated generalizations. He was exact. I'd seen him pick individual salt grains off a pretzel and eat each one. "You don't mean everyone," he said.

"Everyone."

"Even though you probably only have a cold?"

"Everyone," I repeated. I was in no mood for probability formulations.

"When I don't feel well, I just don't want to miss work," he said. "I'm not thinking about dying, so I'm not sure you can say everyone."

I believed him, and I swore to him that I had misspoken.

I knew he considered sickness a mistake which should be ignored. He apologized to anyone who would listen if he missed his daily run because of a fever. But I couldn't believe we were having this conversation when all I wanted to do was sleep.

When I next woke up, Gina was on my bed. More precisely on my achy chest. Terri was standing over us.

Gina asked, "Why Will ni-night?"

"He's just lazy," Terri told her.

"Will want dinner?" Gina asked me.

"Breakfast, sweetie," Terri corrected. "It's still breakfast time."

"No thanks," I said.

"Gina want breakfast," Gina said.

"What are you having?" I asked her, trying to sit up for the first time that day.

"Hotdog, apple juice, french fries, ice cream, candy," she listed.

"Anything healthy?"

"No," she said, quite pleased not to know exactly what I meant.

She was chubby and attractive as she jumped down, graceful in the slow movements of her fingers around a Sesame Street toy. She crouched like a catcher, but easily, her pyramid feet solid, and put Big Bird on the end of her thumb.

"Do you think you have a temperature?" Terri asked.

She had a particularly nice way of touching my head, gently and unhurriedly. She brushed my hair back. My eyes burned, my throat swelled.

"Does it matter?"

"You're not going to die. You're really not."

"So I hear."

"A day in bed. Boy, does that sound good to me," she said.

At that moment it sounded good to me as well. Shep had taken the older kids skating. It was just me and Terri and Gina.

"Gina. Go get me three eggs and pancakes, bacon, hot chocolate," I said.

Gina ignored me, piling puzzles and Little People and Sesame Street dolls around my bed.

Then she said, "Will read book."

I had tea and toast with tangy marmalade and I read about eight books to Gina who didn't believe in the germ theory and kept leaning her face against mine to see better. Then Gina brought me the automatic control and said "Push clicker," while I changed television stations until we found one she liked. Sesame Street. It was just after 9 A.M.

Terri came and sat with us, pushing us over to one side, taking her shoes off and crawling up onto the pullout bed that sagged deeply where Gina sat on my knees blocking the picture. Terri had beautiful eyes and long bottom lashes. I didn't hear the TV but I seemed to hear everything else, a clock in the next room, alarms faraway, kids outside screaming, banging, faking laughter. Also creaky noises in my ears. My mind wandered. I started thinking about Sara and how I had not seen her since at the Sidelys', except at a distance down a school hall. I had thought of calling her once or twice, and prayed that she'd call me, but it didn't seem to work out. I missed the way her Adam's apple moved and the way she made muscles with just this little wave happening where her bicep was. Outside, the sky was flat gray. No matter what season it is, it feels like winter when you are sick.

"When I stayed in bed sick as a girl, I used to smoke. Even though I knew it was bad for me, I did it anyway. That stream coming out of my mouth made me feel healthy," Terri said.

"Your mother must have loved that."

"My mother never believed I was really sick, so it didn't matter."

I told her that as far back as I could remember, when I was sick my mother usually set me up for the day—magazines, games, television—but went to her job. She would call twice during the day, usually waking me, to check how I was feeling. Most of the time she came home at her regular hour.

Terri disappeared for a few seconds and came back with a washcloth in her hand. "Kenny likes this," she said.

She kneeled, leaning over me, her hip just touching my arm, and laid the cool washcloth over my forehead for a moment. Then slowly she rubbed it along my face, over my closed eyes, stopping at the temples. Across my chin, its roughness was surprising. I felt myself loosening. My rib bones cracked a little bit, or I thought I heard them crack, and my nose tingled and the room felt hotter. Gina watched Sesame and Terri began talking about the house she grew up in, the wraparound porch and the thirteen stairs up that led to her tiny blue room. I tried to stop thinking because thinking was dangerous. I had the feeling that I wanted to show myself to her and lie as open as the spoon she had used for the marmalade. I wanted to have my underpants off and she would be as eager as I was. When my knees came up in shame and excitement as it grew and I drew my butt tight, Terri gently pressed them flat again, as if she wasn't scared, as if she knew. I wanted it to be Gina's nap time; I wanted her gone to her room with her nappy blue blanket. Then I stopped thinking. My chest was hot and smooth, and Terri's voice was low. Her pretty eyes worked strongly on me. I knew I would be better the next day and I would be able to drive home.

Before I fell asleep again I remember her looking at me with love; it was the first time I recognized that look of hers.

CHAPTER 12

At the end of every basketball practice, at around 6:30, when Coach Bates went back to his little office with the framed certificates, tin trophies, and metal desk with rounded shiny silver corners, a line formed at the top of the key in the suddenly quiet gym. Coach Bates asked us not to do this after practice because he was worried about injuries, but he knew if we didn't get it out of our 16-year-old systems in the clean dry gym, we'd be outside under the lights clearing snow and ice. The cheerleaders, who pranced and did splits in one corner of the gym during our practices, also began to clear out. Their goodbyes were different from Bates's: kiss-blowing, pom-pom lifting, high-kicking, panty-revealing exits. A few had boyfriends among the players and several couples always snuggled during this ceremonial leaving. There were twelve of them and twelve of us, and each girl was assigned to cheer particularly hard for one of us during games. I always felt bad for Iris that she had me. Billy told me that her friends teased her about getting the only white guy, and a benchwarmer at that. But she was cheerful and good-humored when I thanked her for her applause after each game. She had a short afro and her upper lip had a sucking pad like a baby's. I thought she was cute. Billy had Linda assigned to be his cheerleader.

So nine of my teammates lined up at the top of the key, while I sat down on the bleachers with a few of the others—Junior Goff, Kirby. There was no point in humiliating myself and they understood. Down the lane they went, streaming toward the basket, some taking a few dribbles, some curling the ball up into their wrists, others palming it outright, then up, up for dunks. I practiced my dunks on an eight-foot basket, two feet lower than regulation, that was attached to the back of Jim Tuffel's house, just under the gutter. I was an airborne maniac on that hoop, an awesome leaper, Dominique Wilkins, a virtual helicopter. But here after practice, with the rim where it should have been, I was a midget, barely five foot nine with skinny shoulders, skinny hips and brown hair that was so straight and heavy I blamed it for my lack of elevation.

After the first few went in, the gym which was all serious, sounded like a prize fight. Just as divers get marks for their high board techniques, the line of dunk masters got rated by those of us on the side. The best was a 1, or simply the name of that week's best-looking cheerleader. A seven was called a Roxanne, a three was called a Deb, a nine was an Angela, and so on. Rating changes among the cheerleaders depended on subtle alterations in hair, dress, shoes.

After the first round of warm-ups, the dunkers themselves started talking:

I heard:

"Sky for the jam."

"Take that."

"Def defying 360 slam bam jam."

"No problem."

I heard:

"Looky here."

"Face jam."

"Yo, yo, yo."

"That's a dope jam."

"Put out the fire."

Then came the handicaps. The best jumpers took off one shoe, or one shoe and sock, or if they were gentlemen, both shoes and both socks. Then they dunked for the best-looking cheerleader. Billy kept himself out of this one, loyal to Linda. Then they made Junior Goff get out there and try to get rim although he was only five foot seven. Junior swore he could dunk but we knew he was lying. Junior talked all the time and I was about the only one who ever listened. I was the first guard off the bench and he was the second, so we were on the same team during every scrimmage against the starters. After each scrimmage, he would tell me about the moves he'd used on Bobo, even lame moves I'd just seen, but they always sounded good when he described them.

Junior got the rim, but lost the ball on the way up.

Then they all asked me to kneel (as the worst leaper) and bow to them. I gave each one a tumbleweed of lint that I found on the gym floor and we all went in to change, feeling strong and renewed.

*   *   *

My mother was seeing a lot of Mr. Lester Warner, and I realized for the first time she probably had seen him a good number of times before I met him. They seemed too familiar too fast.

One night, Lester decided to take his mother out for dinner and invited us, me and my mother. He picked us up about 5:00, my mother scooting home early from work to put on one of her purple party dresses. Lester drove a clean green Buick which felt as new as a rental car. I could tell he always kept a full tank of gas. He leaned his seat way back and stayed in the left lane at around seventy-five down the Turnpike. My mother seemed genuinely relaxed and listened to him tell a story about some young guy cutting him off once on the turnpike, the two of them pulling off at the Thomas Edison area and jawing it out. Lester said the guy got out of his car and came over to where he was parked with the window rolled down. He got the punk (he called him the punk) so mad that he reached in for Lester and Lester caught him with the automatic window, trapping his arm. Then he began to accelerate. When the guy screamed mercy, Lester let his arm go and drove off. My mother acted unimpressed and called this kind of behavior juvenile, but I was checking out the power in Lester's forearms, in his short sleeves, to see if I'd misjudged his strength that first visit.

We took the Turnpike about 12 exits, deep into New Jersey. The Turnpike stayed elevated through the tough, black cities and settled down to ground level once things got green. We were heading to where Lester grew up and his mother still lived in the church-managed nursing home. The air outside leaked in, rural and sweet-smelling, like Connecticut, even though we were still on the highway. We got off at the $2.65 exit; I was holding the toll pass. When I asked him how close, he said, "When the roads get crunchy."

91

Soon we were in farmlands and Lester was telling how he
grew up in these fields and how his grandfather voted for
whatever political party promised not to put in curbs. He told
about playing high school football without a helmet (never a
good idea, it seemed to me), about his paper routes, about
how chickens put out one egg every day until they are two
years old, except during the winter. He told us about his
dead father. I always listened carefully to those dead father
stories for hints about my future.

My mother must have been nervous, because she asked
him, "Tell me again what she likes to talk about?"

"She's been around the block," Lester said. "Don't be afraid
to talk with her about anything. She's got a few opinions.
She's eighty-eight, but she's planning on at least twelve more
so she can get a letter from the President."

"But what does she like to talk about?"

"She likes to hear what's happening in other people's lives.
She likes to hear about the world. I don't know. She'll tell you
a thousand recipes. She's really not a bad old egg," Lester
said.

I saw muddy fields and farm posts and crummy shacks
and knew that we were heading back in time generally when
we pulled up in front of a small red-brick building on a wide
street across from some tennis courts. It had no name over
the entrance, but it did have a ramp with a rail.

We all went in. The entrance area was empty, there were
a few pictures of snow scenes on the walls along with a brass
crucifix, and we headed toward a small office to report our
arrival. My mother seemed nervous and she tried to hook
arms with me but I avoided her. A slender woman with gray
hair and watery eyes led us down a hallway where many very
old people sat on benches, canes and walkers planted in front
of them, eyeing us like a jury. I smiled at them, nodded, and
said hello, but my mother would not give them a look. I knew
that old people were mean and bitter but I gave them the
benefit of the doubt. We found Mrs. Warner's room, a remov-
able plastic nameplate beside the room number.

She was tiny, gap-toothed, and full of energy. Lester introduced my mother first and they shook hands almost sur-

prised to be seeing each other. Then I took her mothy hand and said, "Nice room."

"They wouldn't let me keep anything from the house. They *discourage* that. So here you have it." She had a few dolls on a scarred dresser, the bed, the TV, and a closet. Old women love dolls; I'd seen them at the houses of half my mother's friends.

Lester said, "Ready?"

She walked fine. Her glasses were held together with a paper clip. We got to dinner all still friends.

She asked Lester to order for her and proceeded to interview me about school, where I lived, when my father died. I spoke loudly but probably didn't have to. Then she asked Lester lots of questions about his new job as distribution manager at Xerox. She avoided my mother, who was as silent as I had ever seen her. Lester was respectful toward his mother and I was wondering if, when I became fifty and my mother was ninety, I would like her any better then. The way adults spoke of their parents in private and then the way they got along with them in public was evidence that my chosen style would not become outdated as I got older.

My mother could handle liquor and hot sauce and she had cornered the hors d'oeuvres. Me and Lester kept the old girl lively, talking to her about some of the vacations they'd gone on together.

"My parents used to take me two towns over to a hotel that had a pool, for our vacations," I told them.

"Sounds chintzy," the old girl said, surprisingly. I could never tell if old people were joking because their voices stayed the same.

"It was fine," I told her.

"I don't believe you," she said.

"It was always relaxing," my mother interrupted. Her shoulders had shrunk.

"Lester, remember we took a camper with that boat on the back and drove to Michigan one summer," his mother said.

"Michigan's wonderful," my mother got in. "I went there once in college."

"I never went to college," Lester's mother said, "and the bungalow we had was shabby."

"But we had fun," Lester said.

Lester looked worried that my mother and his mother were not becoming allies.

We sat for a while and I saw Lester trying to make out the sporting event on the television hanging over the bar halfway across the room. His mother sat up straight, all business, while my mother kept adjusting her blouse, jerking one shoulder down, then the other as if she never bought the right size clothing.

"You a good cook?" Mrs. Warner asked. "My son likes good cooking."

Before my mother answered, Mrs. Warner went on, "He likes it well done. And don't hold back on the gravy either."

"Never," my mother mumbled.

There was a meat smell everywhere as the plates of food arrived under metal hoods.

"Now, you say you do social work, do you?"

"Yes, that's right."

"People think of social work as 'good' work, but I don't equate the two necessarily. I've heard enough stories of people getting forced into things, getting led to make decisions they regret later, by social workers. After all, social workers are just trying to make things go smoothly, the results be damned, aren't they? Social workers might not even mean good at all, isn't that right Lester?"

Lester was off in the hockey game he was straining to see, but he managed, "Absolutely right, mother. But you happen to be sitting next to one social worker who does mean well."

"Tell me one good thing you did today," she said to my mother, her crooked, skinny fingers jabbing the table.

My heart was pumping and I hadn't even tasted my roast beef served with extra blood, roasted potatoes, and green beans. My mother's lips were sour. She gave Lester a save-me look and avoided my stare altogether. Lester said nothing.

"I deal with children mostly," my mother began.

"Sad. Sad," Mrs. Warner muttered. "But it's your funeral." And then she started eating in a methodical, old person's way.

When I met very old people, I expected them to offer me a lesson in life, something I was bound to disagree with. But Lester Warner's mother only wanted to raise a little hell with my mother. I sort of enjoyed seeing my mother squirm, but at the same time I felt she had made an honest effort at being friendly and didn't deserve to have her scrod ruined.

I realized that Mrs. Warner was peppy because she had a bad temper and didn't put it to much use in the home.

We skipped dessert, Lester saying, "You better watch your sugar," and we got out of there. We dropped her off, my mother not getting out of the car but mumbling goodnight through the window. If the old woman had reached her hand in, I'm sure my mother would have put up the auto window on her. Luckily my mother had a bad memory and wouldn't remember most of the dinner.

I thought about how Lester, for all his good will, ditched his mother and how my mother had ditched me, Lester for his purposes (his mother couldn't have wanted to move into the home), my mother for her purposes. And yet, there was Lester acting chummy with his mother after calling her a fuddy-duddy, and my mother acting close with me, at least in the beginning. Bitter facts had been ignored, it seemed to me. I almost asked Lester if he loved his mother, but the answer would have been worthless. I was thinking, as we headed up the highway, what my mother would be like at that age, fenced in and furious, after I'd put her away in one of those idiot parks. I was wondering if I could begin to hold this threat over her starting immediately.

CHAPTER 13

The day after I met Lester's mother, I drove back to Connecticut. On our Saturday evening walk, Terri asked me, "Do you love your mother?" Crazy question, Terri trying to rev me up, right in the middle of a perfectly good conversation about T-shirts.

"What do you mean by that?"

"Do you love her?"

"You mean do I think I can say I love her?"

"That's one way of avoiding the question."

We had walked the green fairway down from the dorm to where the woods made a halo around the lake. We headed along the trees, the dark body of the lake on our left, the dusk a pollen yellow. In the house, Terri seemed nervous and I always felt protective of her. I had heard her turn down plenty of invitations from other faculty wives to dinner parties and lunches, claiming she had too much work. She seemed alone too often. Down by the lake on these walks, we talked about ourselves and let the other person drill away at our silliness. There was the smell of old leaves and I was usually very happy talking about our secrets, mistakes, and our common worries.

I liked Terri because she took me seriously. Sara took me seriously, but she was only my age. Also, I didn't see her anymore, except occasionally and awkwardly at school.

"My mother has too many pleasures," I said.

"So you can be mean to her because of them?"

"She likes her ice cream and popcorn and vacations and boyfriends."

"Which is why you never eat dessert."

"Which is why she's absurd."

I remembered my mother telling me recently that I was unaffectionate. Her saying this surprised me—not that I

96

wanted to rush over and hug her out of remorse—but that she could tell I avoided her seemed remarkable. Then I realized it shouldn't have been remarkable; she wasn't stupid.

"I remember my mother wanting me to be the goose girl when I grew up," Terri said. "She wanted it more than she wanted anything for me. More than she wanted me to go to college or have a job or children, or get married."

"Go ahead, what's the goose girl?" I asked, sounding bored.

"Where I grew up in California, in the center of the raceway at Hollywood Park, there's a pond. You know, my father, after work, sat in a ticket window at Hollywood, cashing bets."

"He did? You never told me that." I expected Terri to tell me everything, and that something had slipped by was a sign of her inattention.

"The Cash Man, his friends called him. He was a track maniac. On weekends, when he wasn't working at the track, we all had to sit in the living room on the red rug listening in silence to the radio during the races."

"I'd love to go to the track," I said. "I've got a system."

"No you wouldn't. Not if you went all the time like we did. My mother had gotten hooked too, or at least knew the vocabulary and acted excited. So, in the center of the track was a pond with ducks and geese and a boat that circled all afternoon every afternoon during the races with that one lucky girl perched in her seat using the oars once in a while."

"The goose girl."

"The goose girl." Terri laughed and looked tired. "The goose girl was the prettiest girl in the area and it was a great honor to be chosen by the pageant committee to ride around in that boat for the summer."

"Did they pay you?"

"You got to meet the jockeys after the races."

"Big thrill." I sounded uninterested, but I loved horse racing on TV, the announcement of the winners' shares, the final payoffs and also just seeing the muscular funny-named sprinters (imagine naming a pet Astroturf). I skipped the trotters on the local stations. They seemed Amish to me pulling their wagons.

"That's what my mother wanted for me."

"You know how you know what a person thinks of you?" I

asked. I thought I was sticking to the subject, but Terri looked annoyed that I wasn't following up on goose-girls.

"How?"

"By what presents they give you at holidays and on birthdays. My mother doesn't give presents. I haven't gotten a present from her in years. That's what she thinks of me."

"That's lousy."

I appreciated when Terri let me go into these self-pity streaks and let me come out of them on my own. I came out of them thinking: I should be thankful my mother isn't home much to bother me.

We walked back. It was dark and the stars were multiplying. At the dorm, Jerry was pulling apart a caterpillar on the floor, his sisters gathered around scared of the broken-off pieces. Gina said, "Look, green pajamas," while Jerry flipped it back and forth, its black, eager suction cups searching for ground.

I slept on my back at the Keans'. It was the only place I was able to fall asleep looking upward. In this position, I felt that I wouldn't miss anything and I was able to listen better to the mumbling in the adult bedroom, and the rare car on the perimeter of the campus. I could have been home on a Saturday night like this, riding the town low in the backseat of a car, one foot hanging out a window. A normal Saturday night for a teenager in America, but here I was alone on a fold-out bed with lousy springs in a family's apartment in northwest Connecticut. Weird. The peepers were going crazy outside, long low sounds like when you hear motorboats underwater. There was a little light that broke over the window frame from the British couple that lived downstairs who were barbecuing meat beside their tomato garden.

When I was nearly asleep, I heard someone walk softly by my bed, past the fireplace where the marble was loose, and out into the back study. It was Shep in a bathrobe.

I tried to remember how Shep and Terri met and came up blank. I wondered how she had chosen Shep. I never asked. Each time we came home from our walks I thought I understood. Shep was reliable. If he didn't know how to do something he would figure it out. He was proud of his accomplishments. When I saw him caring for the kids sometimes it was obvious to me why Terri loved him. Yet at times her body didn't seem to respond to his, like mine did with Sara's or Sara's did with mine. Watching them, as Shep kissed her and she kept her hands in her pockets, I figured this was how love was, or at least marriage. As Billy said, "Lust, rust, dust." Sometimes, I wanted to push Shep and say, "Notice her like I do."

When I talked with Shep, our conversation was always upbeat. He checked *Scientific American* for probability problems for me. He told me about the conference he had just attended to "keep current" on Medieval Europe, although keeping current on the Middle Ages of course made no sense to me. He read me a great quotation he'd just found in Bartlett's. All in his jittery, lively way. But that night, he slipped past me, quietly, and I didn't stop him, and tell him I was awake, like I would have if it had been Terri.

In the morning after breakfast, Shep and I went food shopping, leaving the others behind. We drove into town in the rain, the air the flavor of apples. Shep talked about how to keep flowers alive in a vase, and swimming in cold water.

"I used to hit the pool at 6 A.M. at every Army base I was ever on. And you know what? The pool was always crowded," he said.

"When were you in the Army?" I asked, doubtfully.

"I wasn't. But you know my father was an officer and we moved around, so I swam in a lot of pools."

"You never told me that." And Terri never told me about being a goose girl. There were too many surprises happening.

"That I was an Army brat? Of course. The army is like prep school, a constant sense of summer and youth," Shep said. "That's why this is all so familiar to me and it would be so hard to change."

The supermarket was small and made for rich people, with nothing marked down and lots of asparagus in the vegetable section. Not one shopper had a beard. Shep pushed the basket and bought carefully. He said hello to two people. I followed him around, touching the foods I would have liked, just to touch them. He thought he was giving me theories of life.

"If you must forecast, forecast often. That's one I like for you," he said. "It's really talking about probabilities," he said, taking Boston lettuce and stuffing it into a clear bag.

"It's about weather," I said.

"And other things."

"Here's one that's really about probabilities. And how life should be. J. Paul Getty said it. 'Rise early, work hard, strike oil.'"

"I guess he struck oil," Shep said.

Shep stopped in front of the flowers, bunches stuffed into tall green plastic containers. He stopped, looked, didn't even sniff, and walked on.

"That's how I felt when I met Terri," he said.

This sounded like a serious non sequitur. I didn't like it when he spoke about Terri to me; whatever answer I gave, I felt disloyal. So I kept quiet. We were almost through the checkout line.

"Like I had struck oil," he finished.

He had one bag and I had one bag. We walked through the sliding electric doors and got to the car where he balanced his bag on the roof while reaching into his pocket for the keys. He said, "You know Terri's leaving."

"For New Haven?"

"I don't mean tonight."

I felt my throat getting dry and tight.

"She's moving out," he said. Then he screamed it, right outside the grocery, "Out!"

I got real quiet and still like a deer when he hears a human voice.

"Can you believe it?" he screamed again. This time I could feel people staring. He was screaming toward me, but looking past.

"No," I whispered.

"You must have known," he said to me.

"No."

"She told you, didn't she?" Then he mumbled, but I heard it because I was listening so hard, "She tells you more than she tells me." I had always thought this was true, and it had always made me feel superior to Shep. That he was stupid and not paying attention to someone who was really wonderful. That Terri did not belong to him. But now I thought: She didn't tell me a thing. I felt as unloved as he must have felt, or how I imagined he felt, although I immediately felt disloyal again, taking his side.

"When things get bad, sometimes they have to stay that way," he said. He lowered himself into the car, reached over and opened my door, signaling for me to pass him my bag. Then he bounced it over his shoulder into the back seat, the food flying. We drove home in silence.

When I got back to the Keans' apartment, I packed. Terri was out with the kids. I thought of how Terri and I talked, too much and too little and maybe to no purpose. I wondered why she never told me about Shep. Maybe she thought I would tell him her secret, or that I couldn't handle it.

Shep came in carrying the grocery bags. I said goodbye, thanks. He looked at me and said, "See you. Be careful on the way."

Fast getaways are important sometimes. But I had a two-hour drive to puzzle over what had happened to the visits that I had come to take for granted. Shep quickly grew small in my mind as I drove, and Terri rose up. At first, I felt badly that I had left without saying goodbye to her. She was always preaching to me about old-fashioned manners. But then I began to wonder why Shep was the one who told me about matters between them in this instance. He and I had never shared such private subjects before. Which led me to think that Terri had other things to tell me.

Perhaps there was another man she was seeing. Maybe her dreaminess was already attached to someone else. Maybe Shep's telling me was just his way of being brave about getting deserted. Or else Terri had asked him to tell me in order to stir up the least trouble in my sixteen-year-old, already suspicious mind.

But if there was not another man, where would Terri go? I automatically assumed she would move out. After all, he worked there, and she always complained about the place. There were probably twenty possible places for her to go to, but I couldn't think of one. I noticed the speedometer at about 80 mph, and then I noticed I was squeezing the steering wheel as hard as a trophy, and I took my foot off the gas and tried to relax.

I was unwilling to think that I would not be back at Winston again. Although I heard about divorce all the time on radio, TV, in the talk of my mother's friends, and I knew that 50 percent of American marriages ended in divorce, I had always believed that actually some 10 percent of Americans found each other, got married, then divorced, over and over in permutations of that 10 percent, thus making the 50 percent statistic as deceptive as my father had always taught me statistics could be. Terri and Shep would not get divorced—there were other options. And three children.

My parents' marriage was the only marriage I had seen close up before Terri and Shep's, and that one had also ended badly for me. As I entered New York State, picking up the Taconic Parkway and reading the name of the new governor painted over the old governor's on the welcome sign, I thought: Maybe that's the way it is with people, one name getting painted over another. I felt like talking with my father. He was gone but I could still talk with him. I told him that I barely remembered the details of his marriage, but I was going to ask my mother. I wanted to ask my father why he married her; was she beautiful then, happy with love, fidgety, foolish, classy? I wanted to know who I was going to ask for advice when I considered marrying. I wanted my father to know that I would have asked him if he were around, but he wasn't going to be around and I was sorry I'd never be able to ask him anything directly again, but that talking to him like this helped. I told him that my fear was not for Terri only, but for myself. I didn't want to lose my weekends of getting trounced by Gina and Jerry, getting fed, and of talking with Terri, of lying in bed listening to the sounds of others sleeping.

I drove the rest of the way home in a rain that had become stubborn and powerful. I thought of Sara's round arms and the taste of her mouth, her brown hair and cheerfulness. Of her breasts in a blue dress I liked. I tried to think of greater things, to figure Terri and Shep out, but I had a meager knowledge of love.

CHAPTER 14

The next day I cut every class until math. I only wanted to see the geniuses, to know that the world was the same, at least for them. They were dependable. Jesus, the guys in my math class were good. They were the same guys I had been with for years. A trace of merit was allowed back into the "everyone is equal" democracy our school had become and the geniuses were given their own class. Each year they were even better—math Olympians. Jesus, what a bunch of freaks, dreaming at the blackboard. By the time I reached Volpo's class, I couldn't really keep up anymore and I veered into probability (which gave me my own angle) and basketball. Mr. Volpo sat in the front, off to the side, at his desk. He looked like a beer distributor, with a little extra weight under his chin, graying hair, and aviator glasses. During the rare times he walked to the board, he had a limp, the left knee not bending. I trusted, for no good reason, that he had a generous streak under his never-worried, slightly disgusted demeanor. I trusted this because he seemed to love math as much as we did. Also, unlike the other teachers, he never wore a sport coat.

The geniuses were the only high school kids I ever met who weren't part-time vandals. They had no interest in half-truths. Dakin, for instance. In eighth grade, I watched him come out of an integral clean. I saw him think magically and angelically. His brain was enormous. Crazy Dakin, who took any dare outside of math class. Jump into the deep end of an empty pool without shoes on. His body was a bullish, knuckle-scraped wonder. Dakin had a sweet spot for me because he liked my father, because my father liked him. Dakin, the crazy underdog, fighting his way out of the belief he was a freak. My father liked him before I did, the two of them talking on the street about how to make a bomb, Dakin age

10. Billy and Dakin had had nothing to do with each other since a fight in first grade that both remembered winning.

I told Dakin the story of my mother's plan to move out even before I told Sara. He told me, "You can't be sure of anything."

"You think she won't do it?"

"Chances are better than you think."

Since Dakin was basically after truth all the time, I weighed his answer into my probability equation about my mother. Probability was of course not fact, but I liked things pinned down, and calculating about my mother was an antidote to cynicism. Dakin gave me this opinion on his sixteenth birthday. I found him after math class and brought him a brownie with a candle in it. With my mother gone more and more, I had been thinking about my father a lot and he would have wanted me to be nice to Dakin.

"Make a wish," I said. So he pressed his eyes closed until his face was as flat as monkey's, then he opened them and blew the candle out.

"You only get your wish if you eat the candle." I couldn't resist. I knew he would do it.

Cerise was 12.5% of our math class of eight, but she made up 100% of the girls and blacks in our little group. She was the third tallest (but Harry and Cal were skinny as minus signs), she had skin the color of chick peas, and her teeth were perfect. Her hair had a wave at the shoulder. Cerise was exceedingly quiet. Mr. Volpo never made her speak; he called on everyone but Cerise, and when she volunteered answers (she only got involved when the problems were most difficult), she whispered huskily. She occasionally got some solutions wrong, unlike Dakin who was never wrong. I put her about third best in the class. None of us were really friendly with Cerise. We had to be respectful of her because of the way she was, but we didn't quite know what to say to her.

Before class, the geniuses talked about the board games they played after school everyday at one of their houses. They were World War games with complicated rules. From what I gathered, blocks represented armies, colors defined nations; (they invited me to play once and gave me a copy of the instructions, but it would have taken me a week to learn the rules so I didn't show). Six dice dictated all allowable maneuvers. The geniuses were ferocious in their Hush Puppies before class. They ranted on and on about mutual destruction, diplomatic initiatives, combat readiness, withdrawal of troops, military assessments. They said things like "We'll be ready to do whatever we're called on to do." Each week brought different alliances. They were serious. I imagined the actual game as a religious ceremony of some sort that could not be exactly described to outsiders.

Dakin and I sat and talked about his latest adventures while the commanders met and Cerise sat alone opening her neat notebook to the latest equations. He would tell me about getting drunk, or climbing down a manhole and exploring the local sewers, or helping someone customize a car, or almost losing a thumb setting off fireworks. His stories were incredible but knowing him, I believed them all. I was sure he never slept, which gave him extra time to entertain himself. I knew he never studied, leaving him unprepared for every subject except math which he understood instinctively.

I never really had a full conversation with Cerise even though she lived in my neighborhood two blocks behind us, the only black family around. I sometimes saw her walking with friends in the evening but they were not kids I recognized and I guessed that they were from other schools. Somehow I knew that her father owned a company and her mother was a lawyer. When she moved in, the man who owned the house across the street from the Powers brought a lawn chair out and watched her house all day long, even having his meals out there. Just sat in his front yard silently watching to see something exceptional for about two weeks until he gave up and went back into his own house. Billy said that none of his friends at school messed with Cerise. The girls said she was a snob and the boys thought she was too tall and funny-looking. In other words, they were scared of her big brain.

If I passed her on the street with her friends, she was polite and would tell them I played basketball, and then she would ask me if our team won recently and by how much and against whom. Her questions demanded short answers.

When I first got to know the Keans, I decided to approach Cerise before math class one day and ask her if she ever considered going to prep school. In some ways, I thought a school like Winston would appeal to her, I'm not sure why. I thought this subject would bring us to a new understanding.

Cerise told me, "I visited Madeira, Miss Porter's, and Concord, and found the infractions they specified particularly gratuitous."

Which I assumed meant no little boarding school uniforms for Cerise in the near future. She never even asked me why I asked.

CHAPTER 15

Probability theory gives you some idea about your chances of success or failure, but it gives you no idea about time, or about how fast things can go wrong. I had lost in a relatively short time Sara and Terri. I had obviously missed something with Sara and I had missed something with Terri too. Had she and Shep really been fighting that much? Maybe a few arguments, but no real knockdowns. I wanted to call her up and ask, "Was I the only one having fun?" But Shep said that she was the one who was moving out. Maybe he had that backward; it was more likely that he was leaving. She wouldn't leave her Kenny and Gina and Clare. Still, I didn't call. I didn't know who to call, or where. Which left me with Billy and of course my mother, whose friend, Lester, was now a regular.

When Saturday morning came, I called Billy.

I said to him, "Billy, I'm out of Connecticut."

"Never been there," he said.

"You know. My friends I visit every weekend." I had been thinking a lot about Terri in a head-shaking way.

"Yeah, yeah, the good woman and the skinny guy. Get a new girlfriend, will you?"

The week before I had told Billy about Sara souring on me. He liked Sara a lot and he said he planned to date her now that she was free. I said she still had a boyfriend and he laughed. That was certainly no problem.

"I don't need a new girlfriend now," I told him.

Billy said, "Find one who can take your underwear off without unzipping your fly."

"You're disgusting, but I approve," I told him.

He invited me over, I put on jeans and a STAMP OUT UGLY shirt, and drove to his house. About halfway there the houses began to look sad, with wooden fences like you'd see in a barnyard, two uneven horizontal bars, rather than the crisp picket of my neighborhood, and by the time I saw his house on its dead-end street, the fences were dog-run wire enclosures, with weeds and exotic flowers growing up them. Billy's house was one story and clean, with gray vinyl siding and window boxes that his mother worked on every day. She grew tomatoes instead of a front lawn, said it reminded her of North Carolina.

Billy's father was as dead as mine. He had been reffing a highschool game when he went over backward like he was taking a charging foul on his own chest. When he hit the wood, he was gone. Billy was twelve, a year younger than I had been. A year younger meant his memories were more out-of-date than mine. On the other hand, his mother had taken the attitude of "we're going to get through this to- gether," while mine started dating immediately. She couldn't help herself.

There were woods behind Billy's house and a basketball court a block away, really two full-length courts where the summer league was played. The courts were green, painted on red macadam and the nets always looked new. The back- boards were clear plastic with a white box over rim level to give some depth. Professional-looking. Dr. J in his prime could pick a twenty-dollar bill off the top of the backboard to win a bet. Billy could get rim (he was long and had syrupy arms) and would have been able to dunk if his hands hadn't been so small, and I could smack midnet if I really tried.

We had become friends at the summer league nearly three years before. I was the only white to have signed up for the league in this part of town. The only other whites in atten- dance were college scouts, and no one messed with them or there would be no scholarships. I hadn't really grown yet and I still had a little fat on me, so no one found me threatening, but I could dribble and was quick for about five steps. I also never missed an open shot. Billy was already a star, his top of the key casuals playing string music. I saw him play in the game before my first game. I think he scored 39. He stayed around to see the next one and I hit for fourteen, and my teammates liked me because I set them up with reverent bounce passes.

Billy came up to me afterward.

"Not bad," he said.

"You bet."

"What's your name?"

"Sterling."

"As in silver," he said.

I was pleased to be talking with him.

"Where's your father at?" he asked. "He ain't here watching his bad boy burn."

My mother had driven me over and fled.

"He's dead."

"You want a drink?" he asked without flinching, and walked off, me following, and I didn't hear that his father was dead until after dinner that night, after his mother stopped blabbing about parking fines and tomato crops and Easter while Billy and I ate about six meals in one. Our identical misfortunes and our near identical basketball talents (I wish) made us cozy.

It took us a while to start talking about girls. Mostly because his were black girls who I didn't know so well, and mine was a white girl he didn't know so well. We were still talking about girls, mostly Billy giving me lessons that were absolute and unknowable. He would show me his fingertips, palm up, and say, "Touch these," as if everything about him could be found in those soft sponges that I already appreciated for their ballistic accuracy. Billy called girls he didn't like "gulp-throats" and he blamed diet soda for messing them up, while his choices had tapered ankles, big butts, and fine, soft-looking shoulders.

Billy had no time for my whining about losing Connecticut or Sara. We went out and shot around as usual. He was talking about his new Linda and her black bras and bikini underpants and I kept thinking about Sara with her top and bottom buttons undone on my favorite blue shirt, but I didn't say a thing because I didn't know really, in any deep way, what went on under, say, her pants. Billy related everything to sex and I cheered him on, ignorant as to the details.

I remembered the summer before when Billy, already sixteen and with a license, had taken a job driving a Salvation Army truck. He picked up old, overworn clothes at people's

houses who couldn't make it into Salvation Army central. He
had pickups out in the country and he always made them
his last stop of the day. His last stop one Tuesday was about
a mile out of Sedonville and owned by an old woman. The
house was packed with piles of old junk—newspapers and
sheets—from the floor to the ceiling. There were narrow
aisles you could walk through, like a labyrinth. The lady had
on an apron and a long green work shirt, Billy said, and the
house smelled of cat. She said the clothes he had to get were
in the basement and when he went down the stairs, she closed
the door and locked it.

It took the Salvation Army two days to find him, after
realizing he hadn't returned the truck. They tracked him
from house to house along his route that last day and when
they rang the crazy lady's bell, she came to the door and told
the men that Billy was in the basement. She had been passing
slices of cheese to him under the door. Billy said he hadn't
really been scared, although I tried to get him to admit it. I
remember when I asked if he had any idea why she did it,
he said, "She probably just wanted some nooky." And that
was it. Billy and sex.

Playing ball with Billy just made my longing for Sara hurt.
My balls jiggled and I adjusted them; I kept my voice strong
and certain on every subject. But he knew it was all hollow.
Billy said, "You need distractions. Why don't you put that
math of yours to work and make us some money?"

"Us?" I asked him.

"Okay. You," he said. "Go bet on some horses."

CHAPTER 16

That's why I asked my mother's friend Lester to take me to OTB. I considered it for exactly one hour after Billy's challenge and decided, bring on the horses.

When Lester came in the next morning with my mother and I asked him if he would take me, he started this song and dance about kids betting, and morality and the value of a dollar, and when he was my age, and today's complex world and in midstride he said, "Get in the car, I'll talk with your mother," but of course I hung around to listen.

I thought it was great that me and Lester could just leave my mother for a Sunday afternoon and go betting. She put up about one quarter of a fuss and then probably thought it was good for us to spend some time together. I knew though that she was in some deep, unannounced way disappointed in me, or him, or both of us, for not inviting her. I didn't think she'd be interested (she had never stayed around for any of my basketball games, and neither had Lester), so when she said, "Oh, you two go ahead," we did.

I was too young to go to the track except as a pure spectator, which would have frustrated me, so we decided to go into the city and hang out at Off-Track Betting. Lester's car had a sun roof that whistled as we drove fast across the palisades of New Jersey, crossing the George Washington Bridge with the April sun's reflection stretching down the Hudson toward the skyscrapers on the New York side, the smokestacks and heavy industry on the New Jersey side. Lester had done a little research and located an OTB parlor in midtown. I was grateful that we could share this older man and boy routine in a way that wasn't embarrassing. I had always worried that one of my mother's steadies would want to go for a mystical walk in the woods in order the share his insights about life among the trees. My idea of an insight was a 50-

to-1 pony with a good bloodline in the sixth. Yes, I knew horse lingo. I had done some research too.

I recognized the part of the city between the sleaze strips and the white stones of upper Fifth Avenue because my mother had taken me to the culture quotient of theatre and modern dance until she gave up, having fulfilled what she felt was duty.

Lester started telling me about all the money he'd won at games as we went around and around looking for a parking place on the street. He never called it gambling. He told me about raffles and picking the winning scores at Super Bowls. Then he said, "I've also won a few dimes at poker."

I thought it was time to show him who he was dealing with. He didn't know that I loved playing poker. So I asked him, "How many possible five-card poker hands are there?"

"You tell me," he answered.

"Two million, five hundred ninety-eight thousand, nine sixty," I said. I could tell from his underground smile that he figured I had simply memorized the number from some book, that I had no idea of how to calculate it myself. I didn't know what my mother had told him about my skills.

"Not bad," he said, unimpressed.

So I gave him another, one I had to sit and figure out.

"How many four-letter radio stations can there be with the first letter *w* or *k*?"

This must have seemed sillier to him and therefore less likely that I would have found the answer somewhere. I could see him getting interested.

"Go ahead," he said.

"Thirty-six thousand five-oh-four."

"You know horses?" he asked.

"Nothing to it," I said.

"If nine horses run, there are five hundred and four possible combinations to win, place, and show. All you have to do is pick the right one."

"That's it?"

"You're on your own, but I might give you a tip now and then."

Lester parked in an underground lot. It cost about five thousand dollars an hour so he said we had to win big. With his tie, he was overdressed for betting it seemed to me, but luckily he had on sneakers, like he was interested in speed himself for the sake of his horses.

When we were on the street walking fast, he said, "I had a college roommate whose father owned race horses. This is to tell you how crazy people get with horses. When my friend called his father to tell him he was getting married and give him the date of the wedding, the old man said, 'That's the day I got a horse running at Belmont, I won't be able to come.' Not congratulations or anything. And when my friend asked him, 'You mean you're not going to come?' his father answered, 'Look, how many times are you going to get married and how many times am I gonna get a horse into the Belmont?' The old man had been married six times."

"How many time have you been married?" I asked.

"Just once."

I waited. I had learned not to push older men on these subjects.

"Divorced. After fifteen years."

"You ever see her?"

"Not a chance. I hate her and she hates me and some bad things don't get better." I remembered hearing something like that from Shep the week before.

Lester said, "If you ever get divorced, make sure you have a good lawyer. Boy, I didn't give her a thing. She had nothing coming to her." His eyes got slitty and alive. Then he seemed to stir and catch his own unkindness and said, "You have a girl?"

"Sometimes," I said. Which I hoped left the impression of having unlimited choices.

"Your mother is the smartest woman I've ever known," he said. This left me wide-eyed, embarrassed, and sorry for him. "If she were here, she'd outbet the two of us."

"Maybe," I said.

The OTB had a few men loitering outside it, muttering. There were ripped tickets on the ground and a green awning over the door. The front was all glass so you could see in, the slack men lined up like job applicants. Inside there were counters for reading your program, chest high, a lot of open space, white scuffed linoleum, and TV screens everywhere with numbers and names on them. Not a picture of a horse to be seen.

Lester got us a program. I read about starts, total earnings, and saw the names of farms in Kentucky and Maryland and even my own state of New Jersey. In the corners of this big white room were the betting booths, a mouth talking through a little hole like you were buying a train ticket.

It turned out Lester was a pro. He had some mysterious philosophy about horses, but he also knew handicaps and a few jockeys. He understood post positions. He explained the race sheet to me from top to bottom. When he started explaining about odds I gave him a dirty look.

I had brought along twenty dollars, but Lester did not make fun of me. He bet at least twenty dollars a race. He said things like "The favorite is vulnerable here," and "That horse gives you value for your money." I had random instincts: I trusted the unexpected.

"We're taking this all too seriously," I said after he picked the show horse in the first two races and went up around eighty-five dollars. I was down to sixteen.

"Sometimes I feel very lucky," he said. "I once gave a guy at work ten dollars before he took a trip and said 'Take out some crash insurance for yourself in my name. I feel lucky.' That's how you feel sometimes and you have to go with it."

Lester didn't tell me what happened to his friend, but I guessed. I also got the sense that Lester liked to win at any game he played. I brought up his wife again.

"What did your wife do that you divorced her?"

"Things are never clear until it's too late," was his answer. He wandered off to the window again, his program filled with circlings and jottings. He had stopped explaining things to me. I went over and sat on a stool. All the men looked a little reckless and messy.

Lester came back, his fist packed with bills. "There is no justice in the world," he said. "Thank goodness for that."

"Pick me the next horse from New Jersey," I told him. He checked the program and told me there would be one in the fourth at 20–1. It was called Approval.

"Your mother tells me you are a hotshot basketball player."

"She's never seen me play."

"But she knows from what you tell her."

"Only enough to brag to her friends."

"She doesn't like sports much."

I was starting to get a little annoyed about Lester winning a lot of money, not giving me any good tips, and then telling me the obvious about my own mother.

"She can't even ride a bicycle."

"She was a city girl."

"She doesn't know a down lineman from a down comforter."

Lester was checking one of the TVs for the last race. With his back to me he said, "She's an independent woman." He had lost and looked concerned. I knew he had a son about twice my age. I wondered if *he* had ever been to OTB with Lester. I wondered if he gambled and lost huge amounts. I wondered if he was an athlete and had ever broken a bone.

"Hey, what if you lose all your money?" I asked. This was what I was worried about for myself.

"It's just a matter of zeros," Lester said.

I sat thinking about this for some time while he put his head back into the program. I tried to figure out if he meant you could lose a lot as easily as you could win a lot. Or that whatever was lost could always be replaced. Or that all things evened out in the end. I wondered if this answer had something to do with his ex-wife or whether he had simply gone crazy here in a small room in the middle of a big city.

"The horses are pretty exciting," I said. I was bored and ready to go.

"If you don't do 'em too much. Eventually you'll lose your shirt."

I brought Lester and my sixteen bucks over to the window and had him bet on Approval for me. Lester picked another horse in the race, Sportsrider, to "make it a little fun." I had little desire to compete with Lester mostly because I was worried that his horse would win. I think he bet one hundred sixty. Approval finished fourth and Sportsrider fifth. We both lost. I told Lester I was broke so we left. All that I knew about mathematics was pointless. Probability theory should already have told me that.

I knew I would tell Billy that I had won. The good part

about best friends is that you can lie to them one day, then tell them the truth a day later and they won't hold it against you. Billy would forgive me and say something like, "Take me the next time and we'll get rich," and it would probably be true.

I would tell my mother I had lost. Maybe she would give me a refund.

CHAPTER 17

Twice each season we played St. Agnes, the parochial school that collected lanky white boys with names like Donovan and Stanky and Mahoney and Anastasi and Crim, from all over the county. It was a school that didn't teach its students much, but taught them well about discipline. The Holy Trinity of sports were football, basketball and baseball. St. Agnes didn't have the acreage for tennis courts or a soccer field, or any other sissy, ungodly sports, so they stuck to the big three.

Traditionally, we beat them in basketball on sheer talent although it was always very close when we played at their place. They were tough, red-kneed, red-faced boys with a military hair code and acne on their backs. As a team, they were astonishingly ugly. Their teeth were in fragments, many below the gumline, and their facial scars were always vertical as if they had been clawed. The bleachers at St. Agnes's gymnasium were also nearly vertical. This had two effects: everyone in the stands was forced to the edge of their seats, and fans near the ceiling were still practically at courtside, just up in the air. There were no bad seats at St. Agnes, no faraway or obstructed views. The court was an echo chamber of about 1200 voices, so visiting teams played on instinct and hand signals. It was a snake pit.

Before the first game that we played, I saw two great differences between our sides. Theirs was a team that lived off potato chips and gum, while our players feasted on twinkies and sweet tarts during the off-season. The other difference was that all of their players were white and ours were black, except for me.

The fifth game of our season, about three months before, we'd played at St. Agnes on a Friday night. We were 5–0 going in and 5–1 leaving; we lost by three points. It was the first time in many years that St. Agnes had beaten us. In announcer lingo they "outhustled" us. Basketball is a game of strength and finesse, one of which St. Agnes had and one of which they lacked. Against us, they played defiantly and outhustling us was only a symptom. I got into the game for three minutes at the end of the first half, received an elbow in the left eye and used the other eye to watch the man I was guarding score three straight baskets. Postgame, on the ride home in our cold yellow bus, there was silence. I think even our coach was shocked.

At practice during the week after the loss we talked about how they "won ugly," about how they got all the calls, about their consistently dirty, jersey-pulling, sneaker tripping, elbow-clearing play, about how slow they were, about how disgusting their cheerleaders looked and about how no one liked to touch them when going for rebounds because of the greasy-feeling skin they had. We were inventive in our excuses. Our coach, interviewed in the school paper gave the two reasons all coaches give reporters, "They played a great game. Nothing worked for us." After the game I remember Coach Bates saying to us in the locker room, "You have to live with this the rest of your lives and so do I." We never got down to talking about the reality of the loss; it immediately became mythic. I hadn't played a role in this loss so his statement didn't have the effect on me that it had on some of my teammates. Clay broke a finger punching a locker on the way out.

The truth was, we got in foul trouble early, Alexi and Roland coming out in the first quarter. St. Agnes's irrational faith in rebounds, without our big guys in the game, had a great effect. A last-second, half-court heave by one of their guards fell in after hitting the rim and the top of the backboard, and we headed into halftime down two. They stalled for the entire twelve minutes of the third quarter in which a total of six points were scored. They also had one very fast kid named Gwen (now there was a first name we could have fun with, preparing for the rematch) who got hot shooting from out where God lost his shoes and scored 28 points on Billy.

Billy said to me, "Two things I've learned in my life about white guys."

"Careful," I said.

"You're not included. You're on our side."

"Go on then," I said.

"First, if they sound stupid, they don't necessarily know anything about car engines. And second, if they look like they're slow-footed on a basketball court, they are not necessarily slow-footed on a basketball court."

That week at school was tough on us all. Walking the halls was never pleasant after an unexpected loss. People I hardly knew kept dredging up the events of the game along with their analyses. "You should have half-court pressed them." "Why wasn't Alexi taken out earlier before that fourth foul?" "You guys needed better ball-handling." Others tried to be generous by remembering games from seasons before or even reminiscing about the first game of the season, a win. I heard no one talk of the wrestling team's success or the stunning upset our girls' volleyball squad came up with. There were no distractions. Everyone exploited the St. Agnes loss to feel a little better about themselves: see, even the basketball team got crushed. The guys from the white door, who had sat on our side but cheered for Agnes, saw the contest purely racially. It was the only game of the year that crew attended, and after the loss, if any of our team ventured past the white door, the usual "Get out of here or you're dead" threats were not heard, only, "Nice game against Agnes, boys."

The third week in April our rematch arrived, so that the torture of the previous loss might come to an end. Every player on our team had been in training like a boxer: strict diet, early morning pre-school workout, lots of sleep, no girls. These were all hardships for me except the last, with Sara gone. No one shaved, again not a hardship for me. Our team got grumpy without twinkies. I put extra odor-eaters in my high-tops to look taller.

For the first time, practices were defined by what was forbidden. There was to be no dunking, no between-the-leg dribbling, no behind-the-back passes, no cursing, no nonsense. There was constant drilling, no standing around. I was talking to Billy about my winnings at OTB when I heard Coach Bates say to me, "Clam up, Sterling." Even the assistant coach, Mr. Marino, stood up from his usual bench seat. He never had anything to say to us anyway, his job was to scout other teams. He smoked a pipe instead of having a personality. There was not meant to be pleasure at our practices anymore. Practice typically began around 3:30 P.M., giving those kept for detention or extra help (most of our team) time to get to the gym. We started with easy lay-ins, then went into figure eights, a three-man weave moving up and down the floor, ending with the last person coming down the wing getting the lay-up. Then we did some shoot-arounds, two rebounders for five shooters around the key. Everyone was quiet and concentrated. We tried out some new full-court press defenses and came up with solutions to escape these same defenses if they were used on us. After about an hour, we scrimmaged, the first team against the second team. If we on the second team got any kind of lead, the coach went crazy criticizing the starters, calling them "hopeless" and "pitiful" but he also stopped the scrimmage, seemingly to give us all pointers, but actually to make sure the first team didn't lose confidence. We always finished with suicide drills, the twelve of us sprinting the court, squeaking to a halt at half court and then at the far end touching the floor with our fingers, a lesson in quick starts and stops.

Most people who watch basketball have the misunderstanding that basketball is social. It isn't, when practiced at the highest level. You perform as a team, you want to win as a team, but you play only for yourself. You're there to build a reputation. At least that's how Billy and I saw it.

Who were the guns on our team? Well, Billy, who played like music was happening inside his head. Alexi, who was six foot seven, wore his hair in dreadlocks and shot best going to his right along the baseline. Bobo, a high-jumper during track season, a no-technique basketball player however, wild and unpredictable, fast and frightening in the open court, who committed a lot of turnovers.

And of course Coach Bates. He was optimistic, determined to be first, a swaggerer. He had a brave spirit. To inspire us he told war stories. How he had been at Pearl Harbor the day before the invasion but had a vacation pass off the island the day the bombs fell, and how his buddies died so he could be here coaching us, a lucky bastard, alive, making us all better players. No matter how many times he told us this story, it had a larger-than-life appeal to me. My teammates feared him because he also taught them history and their grades depended on good scoring outputs.

We had no trainer on our team like the professional teams have. Before the game no one got treated, taped, massaged, or soaked. We warmed up our own muscles. Mine were cold before the St. Agnes rematch on Thursday. I'd been cold all day. Every time I felt my fingertips they were like ice down to the second joint, and I had to tuck them under my thighs as I sat in class. My nose was cold too, but my underarms were dripping wet, and with my hands tucked under me I felt tiny drops of water running down my arms and coming out my sleeves onto my palms. I got six straight verb conjugations wrong in Spanish and my teacher gave up on me. I couldn't eat lunch. I got colder and colder, the locker room never had enough heat and when I put on my shorts and tanktop Bergenville jersey, I was shivering, my skinny biceps covered with goose bumps.

As we gathered around Coach Bates before taking the court, everyone was looking at their feet. Even Coach Bates. He said only, "Look you guys, put us all out of our misery and beat the hell out of those pansies." We put our hands into a pile, four white ones, mine and Coach Bates, the rest brown, and we chanted "Agnes, Agnes, Agnes," until we were frantic, and we threw our hands up like a dealer losing control of his deck of cards.

I was always glad to leave the locker room. It stunk in there. Sometimes I didn't breathe for minutes, certainly not through my nose. I've heard former coaches turned announcer on TV say what they missed about the game was the smell of the locker room. Yeah, sure.

The court was riotous when we came out. The familiar three lights hung down spaced along the length, three bulbs under three reflectors, leaving an outline of three rings on the floor. St. Agnes was already out at their end, taking lay-ups, ugly, ugly. As we broke into two lines for our own lay-ups, for the first time in a week, we started to speak with each other. Of course it was about girls; that was a good sign. Junior Goff said, "Linda looks fine, don't she?" And Bobo said, "Good as a diploma." We each said something rude about one of our cheerleaders and we were smiling and laughing while Agnes looked tight and very white in the glare. When the buzzer sounded, announcing the start of the game (sounding the same as the one used for our fire drills), we went back to our bench, gathering around Coach Bates. The crowd sounded like one giant stomach that was rumbling.

Coach Bates looked around our circle and said, "You know it."

Then Billy, our captain, said, "Shoot when you see the whites of their thighs."

We broke up with one more hand-flying yell, the starters going out onto the court, the rest of us scattering along the bench. Junior, whom I couldn't take for very long because of his constant bragging, sat next to me, about six down from Coach Bates, and told me that the St. Agnes uniforms looked like pajamas. Against pathetic teams, the bench was a constant stream of side comments and insults about the looks of the other team. But against St. Agnes this time, we concentrated on the action. We were not allowed to call out curses from the bench, so our imaginations were stretched. I yelled things like, "Hey Gwen, nice name! Who's your sister, Lucas?"

Conditioning is all in the feet, and although we had played them before and lost, we now seemed more fit. Alexi won the tap and Billy took it in for the first two points of the game. St. Agnes knew that their chances of taking back-to-back games from us were slim, so they played slowly, zone offense, zone defense, old style basketball like they allowed in the NBA before they brought in black guys and the 24-second clock. St Agnes played the game chest high—no dribbling, no bounce passes—where our speed would not come into play.

I yelled, "Boring. Boring."

Junior yelled, "Bring out an oxygen tent for those guys."

Sweeney yelled, "This is no pension plan. Play like you have legs."

Even our crowd was mean: booing when they took foul shots, clapping at their substitutions. Our guys were running good and fast when they had a chance, but a little too excited, too fast. Bobo was getting sloppier every trip down the floor and Coach Bates was throwing his towel around his head and over his eyes like a swami. After one quarter we should have been winning but we weren't, and the starters looked unsure in the huddle. There was some booing from our side and a few cheers from theirs; the gym had gotten humid and smoky.

In the second period, Gwen got hot again like in the first game. St. Agnes seemed to speed up and we slowed down. Up in their bleachers, parents and stepsisters and nephews and classmates were stomping and craning and shaking their heads. Bobo was jittery and twice dribbled off his feet on breakaways. We were down eight at the half.

In the locker room, democracy was done away with. Coach Bates did not speak in sweet tones.

He said, "I will not stand for this," and "That was unacceptable," and "You are just not goddamn good enough," among other things.

He turned to Bobo and screamed, "What do you think you're doing out there?" and all of us who'd been looking at our feet looked up to see if Bobo would answer, but when he didn't, we stared down again.

Then Coach Bates's voice came at me, "Sterling, you're starting the second half, so tie your sneakers twice, boy."

My mouth got salty and I had a palpitation in my throat. Coach Bates drew a few diagrams while Coach Marino paced and kicked a few lockers for emphasis. We went back out after about ten more minutes of insults and did our lay-ups without much enthusiasm because we were all thinking and saving our energy. I had never started a game or even a half before. My only experience was during the garbage minutes at the end, when the game had already been decided.

As I passed Billy, switching lines during the warm-up, he looked me in the eye and said, "This is business." But I had him smiling too.

When I went out to center court for the tipoff, Gwen came over to me and I extended my hand (we had been opponents once in a summer league game) and he said, "You're a no-playing white motherfucker."

Then he walked away, my hand stranded out there like an empty fishing pole.

During the next two quarters I was informed by St. Agnes players that I was wearing hair-coloring and that I was too pretty to get mugged, while my teammates told me to watch the picks, force them to the middle, switch men, and screen and roll. Billy guarded Gwen and I took their ballhandler. Billy said afterward that I had him like a condom. After about seven minutes my knees unlocked and my fear disappeared and it was a night of freedom. I protected the ball better than Bobo had, Alexi got going, and St. Agnes began to look middle-aged. I was calm, even during the time-outs when I had a moment to think, and the team relaxed. Billy scored fourteen points in the final twelve minutes and we won by nine. I think that they were shocked that a small white guy on a team of blacks could do such damage.

There was one moment I'll never forget. Why is a breakaway so fine? Probably because there is nothing so good as being chased, hearing the heavy breathing behind you, knowing you'll get away. It's like being a child again (I chased Gina at every visit, roaring), even during the pressure of a high school basketball game. But at the far end of a fast break there is also that feeling of leaping at just the right time, from just the right place, of knowing your chaser is tired and heavy and will never go up in the air with you. You are alone except for the flash bulbs and the rim, and the ball rolls off your fingers big as the moon. When you land there is silence. The focus changes and first you see the blue cigarette smoke and you peek around and see the faces, and the red flannel shirts, and colorful banners, and then you hear the crazed room like it's the end of an rock concert.

I'm glad we won, not only for the team's sake, but because the game was good for my reputation. I had beaten St. Agnes and the odds. I didn't even expect to start the next game—Bobo was better than me most days. I never needed to play that well again, ever.

CHAPTER 18

Me and Billy were always trying to think of ways to make money. We each wanted a lot, but were willing to take less if we didn't have to work hard at it. At minimum, we each wanted an indoor basketball court. One of our best ideas, we thought, was to get two well-known, retired basketball pros, Wilt and Kareem, or Dr. J and Larry Bird to play one on one. Rent a stadium and let people pay to watch, five dollars a head. Get a TV contract. Penny-pinch Kareem and Wilt, who really didn't need the money anyway, and keep the rest. We always had one or another plan moving through our heads and were willing to steal new ideas anyone else came up with during our monthly poker game.

Two out of every three times we played at Billy's house. The game started about eight on Friday night and when I knocked on Billy's door it usually opened to his mother standing there pointing me toward the basement entrance just down the hall on the left. Her pointing meant no stops in the kitchen to the right. Don't even think about snacks. Her face was turned away from the pointing hand so I just saw cheek—a traffic cop—but smiling. "They already down there," she always said. "Will, you in no hurry through life, are you?"

I was probably the only one who didn't need to duck going down. I held the bottom, dusty edge of the paneling rather than the squeaky railing as I descended and about halfway down I heard the voices.

"Go figure it."

"Just like I told."

"Fuck you then."

"Go find your purse."

"Forget that."

"Naw. I'm there. Just spread 'em out."

The basement was one big room with black and white tiles like a chessboard. In one corner there was a wood stove with a silver pipe going up through the ceiling, and along one wall stretched a long shelf that held Billy's overflow trophies. There was a tape player on the floor. The room vibrated with enormous sounds. It was cool and smelled of mildew no matter what season it was.

"He's coming," Bobo said. "Put on the music."

I heard the tape get ejected and the click of a new one going in and the hip-hop changed to Barry Manilow's "Somewhere in the Night."

"That's for you, man," Sweeney said. "Now we gave you your music so don't beat us bad."

"Yeah, go easy on us," Bobo said.

Of course it wasn't my music; I hated the stuff. It was the first and only white-boy crack allowed. This was the unstated deal: I did no black gang signs with my fist if I won a hand, tried no fancy interracial handshakes, didn't bob and tip when I walked, didn't use words like "diss," and in return they didn't make me feel like the minority of one I was down there. "An unfortunate difference of color," Billy called my predicament when we were alone.

Royce always tried one white crack after the music routine, but I believed this was because he had patches of white on his hands and face that looked like someone had taken an eraser to his pigment and he felt bad about it—I didn't take it personally. Plus, he wasn't funny and no one felt the need to follow up on his stupidity.

I took my normal seat to Billy's right. Billy said hello by looking at me and lifting up his chin quick, like he'd just taken an uppercut, then dropping it. The chips were black and red like the cards, about dime-size and kept in a brown paper bag next to Billy the Banker. Royce called him the Banker because Billy won nearly every time and also because he was known to use the backboard on most short jump shots. Billy won a lot and I generally lost a little money, never much. The chips cost a nickel a piece, all the same value so no one got confused. Stakes were low because we were all friends, all teammates, and wanted to keep it that way. No big losers. No one had ever tilted the table in cash-poor anger and there had never been a fistfight. In addition to me, Billy, Bobo, Sweeney and Royce, we usually invited a sixth none of us knew quite as well, someone we didn't run with and who we didn't mind beating up on verbally and financially. We all wore gym clothes except the sixth who didn't know any better. The sixth that night was a guy named Siz, short for "sizzle", star center fielder and smart guy.

We each had our favorite games when we dealt. Royce did five-card stud, which led to great loud teasing every sixth hand when one of us grabbed the deck from him saying there was no way he could deal a game called stud. Bobo liked straight poker, Sweeney liked any game with wild cards and Billy always played anaconda and I did too once in a while.

Between hands, there was always lots of talking and razzing. At the table we talked about deodorants, the difference between white and black people's, sprays versus roll-ons, when it should be applied, how many times a day, whether it could adequately replace a shower in most instances. We talked about payday and how fast Sweeney and Bobo spent what they made at Burger King and Kentucky Fried Chicken.

"I wouldn't work at those places if you paid me," Royce said.

"They do pay you," Sweeney said. "I ain't paying you. I'm here to take your money."

"They don't pay enough," Royce answered.

"Enough for what?"

"Enough for me to go missin' time with my girl."

"But then you don't have nothing to buy her nothing with, and we do, which is why we'll be takin' your girl from you."

"I don't think so to that," Royce said.

"You call that bitch right now and see if she ain't goin' out with me tomorrow night," Sweeney said.

"You're crazy," Royce said.

"Call her," Sweeney said. "You two aren't tight as you might think. She's goin' out with me tomorrow in the PM."

"You're crazy. And you better not be seein' Sylvia tomorrow."

Before things got ugly, Billy usually stepped in. It was his house and one of the walls of paneling already had a divot on the basis of a punch from a big-pot loser weeks before. Billy kept his mom away from that wall. I think it was Sweeney who did the damage, losing with three jacks to a full house.

"Can't you take a joke?" Billy said to Royce.

"Never make fun of a guy who's losin'," I added.

The conversation downshifted after exchanges that were tense and we'd talk about the Yankees or the Mets or a basketball player on one of the teams we'd just played, or who would make All-County, or a new video release. We'd talk about how ugly old people are, how their skin gets all glossy and you can see their pores.

We drank Millers and ate Cheese Doodles early and ordered pizza later. We had this routine of back-dunking all Miller cans when we finished them. The floor got sticky and littered, and feet squeaked when someone got up to pee.

Royce had control of the tape deck, including the volume unfortunately. "Hugging music," he called it, Luther Vandross, also some hip-hop. Sweeney was our liar. He lied constantly and everyone knew it. About getting into the Yankees locker room with a friend. About winning three hundred dollars in the lottery. Bobo was the complainer. He always had some physical agony. He had the unbearable pain of a pulled calf. He had the rare and excruciating problem of a popped finger joint. He wanted sympathy. He was brave at cards though. Too brave: he never saw the danger until it was present. He was our regular big loser.

Waistband sweat took over from mildew around 9:30. Billy was already rolling by then, winning his Anaconda every sixth hand. Anaconda was always a big pot: seven cards dealt, a bet, pass three cards to the player on your left, a bet, pass two cards to the player on your right, a bet, pass one card to the player on your left again, a final bet. Four bets and your hand kept changing; nothing was certain except a red and black mountain mid-table. The card changes went well beyond the limits of any probability artist, but Billy always won. The loser was usually a big loser.

When Bobo lost that night, for the third time chasing Billy to the final bet, he kicked over the tape deck. "That thing's bothering me. Shut it down," he said to Royce. Then he bent and rubbed his toe.

Royce said, "The radio's fine. *You* are bothering it and me."

Bobo said, "Can't hear myself think even."

"Maybe it's quiet in there, that's why you can't hear it," Billy said.

I tortured Bobo by making him play Anaconda again, right then.

He smiled through the first card switch, frowned at the second pass, hitched his collar after the final pass, but wouldn't get out and cut his losses. Billy won again, back to back. That's when things went bad.

"Oh, man," Bobo yelled. "Sonofabitch. Shut off that fucking radio." He stood and walked around the table three times, a maniac shaking his head.

Royce laughed at him. "You want to sit out a while?"

"Fuck you," Bobo said.

"You got yer game there, huh, Billy," Siz said quietly. But he said it looking to Billy's right, at me, not directly at Billy. Siz was up about two bucks, but he squinted at me, cold and mean. His little goatee looked sharp.

Billy didn't look at me and I didn't look at him. We each looked at Siz, innocent.

"Two Anacondas in a row. My, my. Sure is your game. Taking it all home. You're getting greedy, Bill, sir."

He had that questioning tone, but no one other than me and Billy were paying attention. Only another star athlete would bother Billy; Sweeney had already announced some wildcard game and was dealing.

I could see Siz's brain setting up hypotheses. I knew that Siz was smart. I knew it the first time I saw him hit. He fouled off about fifteen down the third base line, puffing his chest and smiling at the pitcher each time he stepped back into the batter's box, before slicing a tired fastball into the right field corner for a triple.

"Play the same game all night. Win most. Nothing like a sure thing," Siz said to me again.

"Will will tell you no such thing as a sure thing," Billy said. "He knows the math."

"Knows more than math," Siz said.

Billy and I had never talked about getting caught. But we had grown too certain; only uncertainty keeps people on

129

guard. That is what probability theory should have taught me.

"Anaconda means snake, doesn't it?" Siz asked no one in particular. Sweeney had stopped dealing. The song being played had a frighteningly deep bass. "Pass 'em, pass 'em, pass 'em. Stick your pointy tongue out. Win. We sit here and give up our chips. Even Will Sterling gives up his chips," Siz said. "Tell us, Will, what's the chance that one Banker can win this game every time he deals it? Tell us, Will."

The sound in the room went from stereo to mono. He was talking to me. I remembered Billy once telling me his theory of crime: if you don't want to be a target, you got to move. But I couldn't answer Siz. I remembered that Siz's brother was in jail for armed robbery, and that they were tight, and everyone said a mean streak ran through that family. I pictured Siz coming at me and my body folding up like a crash dummy's. I tried not to panic, tried not to make a dash for it.

"The point?" Royce asked. "Speak English, man."

"No point," Siz said. "You guys play here, I should say, lose here, more than I do. I have nothing to say."

"Say it, man," Bobo said, "Don't stop your shit now."

I could see Siz relax. I could see that he might want to come back some day (he was, after all, up for the evening), and he couldn't be sure. He didn't want to make enemies. He was only guessing.

"Naw. Nothing worth mentioning," he said. He gave a shoulder hitch as if to say, "What's the point explaining this to you dumb fucks who put up with this every month." Then he gave us all a big happy face.

The next song started, and Sweeney finished passing the cards. Bobo said something about there being so much pizza grease on the cards that if you could remember where you dripped it you could play this deck like it was marked. No one picked up on what Siz was implying.

Siz almost had us. He'd come to an insightful conclusion because Billy and I had gotten sloppy greedy. Wanting to win every Anaconda, plus the other hands we won by understanding our opponents and pure luck.

Poker should be gambling, but this wasn't poker for me and Billy, at least not during Anaconda. That's what Siz knew first time out. Billy held his cards upright over the table, leaning forward, and I tipped my chair back to get a good look at his hand. Then I passed him the cards he needed during the three-card and the one-card passes. I always sat to his right. If anyone saw me looking they'd figure, Too bad for Billy, he wins too much anyways. Everybody tried to look at the hand of the person next to him. Billy was just dumb enough to let me look.

I'd stay to clean up the Miller cans and we'd split our winnings. With the Anacondas, we always picked up at least five dollars apiece. Minor league riches, spending money. We liked the danger. Helping, we called it; we never used the word cheating. We never talked about getting caught, but I believed it would be hard for anyone to actually prove, so we were safe. And that's what Billy probably thought also. If worse came to worst, if any of the regulars picked up on our scam, we'd just stop.

It was hard to think about poker without thinking about winning. The two were connected until Siz had his hunch and then let us go. Betting at unguaranteed poker was like lots of other things in my life: the loser would be the person who failed to respond.

CHAPTER 19

I woke up the next morning feeling sore and still tired. I called Terri in Connecticut from the kitchen using the phone next to the cookbooks that my mother never used. Who would give my mother a cookbook as a present? Someone who did not know her or perhaps one of her men dropping a hint.

"I'd like to come visit today," I said. "Maybe we could talk."

"We always talk," Terri answered, not getting it. She was cheery, but I wasn't in the mood. "What time are you coming?"

Then, unbelievably, she wanted to chat, but I was mumbling and she asked me "What time?" twice more before she listened long enough to hear me.

"You okay?" she asked, finally.

"Okay, dokay," I answered, but I changed the time I was arriving to an hour later than I'd first told her.

When I hung up I felt awful and I just wanted to get in the car, get there, and get it over with. Instead, I was irritable and hung around the house most of the day, keeping to the schedule I had given Terri. I checked out the sports pages, opened the refrigerator every hour, always finding it nearly empty. My mother had gone shopping with Lester for some gardening equipment—thick gloves or one of those trowels that looked like a raccoon's claw—and the house was quiet. As the morning wore on, I sat in the under-stuffed chair in my mother's room watching junk on TV and looking into the mirror she used when she plucked hairs off her chin, a two-sided mirror which, when turned over, magnified my face. I thought about the school blood drive that I was avoiding because I was afraid of needles, and I thought of piercing one ear, but that meant a needle too. I thought about whether I would try to avoid Siz at school. I thought about Sara and the way she had an extra hole in her right ear for a second earring.

My mother didn't come home for lunch and I had a can of baked beans with a peanut butter and jelly sandwich. Late in the afternoon I took her car and headed up to Winston, leaving a note on her bed that I realized afterwards read like one of her notes to me: Thought you'd be interested, gone to Connecticut, home whenever.

I was worried in the car. I considered the possibility of getting a flat and I wondered if I would be able to figure out how to work a jack. I wondered if I had enough money to have someone else, a gas station attendant, change it for me. Mostly, I worried about me and Terri. I tried to figure out if it was her fault, or Shep's, but I couldn't, and I couldn't imagine how her life was going to be better than it had been. I wanted to ask her about this but I knew I wasn't going to.

It was a gray afternoon and the road still had a wet strip in the center of each lane from an earlier rain. I looked into the cars of people I passed and saw carseats and curtains, and *Playboy* bunny silhouettes hanging from mirrors. The trees were filling in with leaves and in Connecticut, when I opened my window, the air was heavy and humid.

I stopped off at the Waldorf for a burger. Gert wasn't working. The place was packed at 5:30. All the old people in town had come in for the early bird special, ham and heavy syrup, and they were sitting around with their clouds of white hair, sipping ice tea and squinting at each other, talking about church the next day. The air-conditioning was on, the compressor humming loudly, and I had gooseflesh even before I was served. Reading and rereading the dessert menu to keep my mind busy, I ate fast. The french fries were frozen inside, but I didn't send them back. I decided against dessert and my stomach growled as I cruised up the hill to Winston.

When I pulled up at the dorm, it seemed quiet. I went upstairs and let myself in. I heard some water sounds coming from the bathroom so I knocked on the bathroom door. Terri was on her knees reaching into the tub to give Gina her evening bath.

"Will," Terri said.

"Will," Gina echoed.

"You bet," I said.

"Will, I have something cooking in the kitchen. Could you watch Gina for a second?" Terri asked. She rose quickly and as she walked by she gave me two little palm-open pats on my chest.

As I sat down next to the tub, Gina asked, "Play?"

"Soon," I said.

"Now," Gina answered.

"How about if I throw you down the drain?"

"No," she said, although I was sure she couldn't really understand what I'd said.

"How about if I put some child-eating fish in there with you?"

"No," she told me. "Candy."

"After your bath."

"Now," she said.

Terri came back in and sat down next to me beside the tub. She was wearing a floppy-collared green shirt and tan shorts. When she reached to help Gina grab the soap, I noticed the black strap of her watchband and how thin her wrist looked.

"I don't know what made me think of this just now but I once worked in this kennel," she said. "And these people had left this beautiful white poodle with us. Pure white, you know the kind, with tufts on its head and paws and at the end of its tail. One of my jobs was to let the animals out to eat one by one, and this poodle came out and ate its pebbles and then decided to roll around on the newspaper I had spread on the ground to catch the dropped food. And when the poodle got up, she had newsprint all over her white fur. I could read off her back. I was horrified and I attached the hose, sprayed the dog down, and the place got sopping wet with the newspaper in big globs on the floor. I was fired that night when my boss came in. That's what I was thinking when I saw the floor so wet, I guess."

Didn't she understand why I was there? It wasn't to give Gina a bath or to hear old dog stories. I wanted to know what was happening to this house, to her and Shep, to me and her. She seemed normal, even good-humored. It made no sense.

134

"Time to get out, Gina," she said.

"No."

Terri got up, grabbed Gina under both arms and hoisted her, Gina's legs bending at the hips and knees so it looked like she was sitting in a chair on the way up. She got wrapped in a towel with a little hood. Terri nudged her toward the door.

"No," she said. She knew sleep was soon to follow and had every reason to object. "Melt down," Terri called this part of the evening, Gina disintegrating from fatigue. It was all very cute and touching, but I was annoyed. Just put her to bed, I said to myself. I had to drive home.

But I knew there was no such thing as just putting Gina to bed. Gina got a nightshirt, Gina got a diaper, Gina got her "blanks" to rub under her nose. She got a bottle of milk, warmed, two books, a tour of the whole house with little waved ni-ni's at her typical places: at every mirror, hanging animal, and plant. I knew the whole deal and couldn't stand going through it just then, so I turned down the invitation to help and went to the kitchen to look for ice cream.

I heard the shade pulled in Gina's room, denying her the final twenty minutes of daylight that would have kept her up. I heard the scrape of wood as her door was shut and Terri came into the kitchen.

"I love her, but some nights, I wish I could just put her to bed three hours early," Terri said.

"Why don't you?" I asked.

"Doesn't work that way."

"Lots of things don't work the way they're supposed to." I assumed she'd understand what I meant, she usually did, but that night she didn't, or wanted to act as if she didn't and I realized that around Terri I had always ignored one instruction of probability: assume nothing. But standing against the stove with my spoon angling out of an ice cream carton, I remembered that assuming is a form of disrespect for the laws of chance.

"Let's eat in here," Terri said.

"I ate," I said. I was ready to talk although I didn't know how it would go.

"You can watch me then."

135

She bent into the refrigerator hunting for carrots and cucumbers and lettuce and I stood there, scraping the bottom of the carton, awaiting the arguments to come. She shut the refrigerator and got down a plate. I could see that the house was more of a mess than usual, toys overflowing baskets, dried diaper wipes on the counters, liquid soap containers knocked over. Shutting the cabinet brought down the papers taped to the door, a Little League schedule, a list of Audubon classes for Clare. I picked them up. Pouring French dressing, Terri looked a little out of it, a look I remembered from the first night that I met her.

"I like your haircut," she said.

My hair was short as a doormat; the barber hadn't even used scissors, just went at my scalp with a hand buzzer. I could feel all the bones of my skull.

"Where are those other children of yours?"

"Quiet around here, isn't it?" She paused. "Activities. I hardly know half the time. They're both staying over at friends' houses tonight."

"And Shep?"

"I actually don't know where Shep is. Shep got his own place this week, Will. He's still keeping most of his things here, but he got his own place in Grover. I'm sorry. I'm sorry that he was the one who told you. I meant to, but I wasn't sure of the timing." She was drinking wine. Her salad kept dripping dressing back into the bowl and she tilted her face down a little when she brought the fork to her mouth.

"He told me you were moving out," I said.

"I'm not moving out. And I wouldn't know what he told you. What he told you was wrong, or maybe it was what he wanted to believe. But he was wrong."

She actually sounded tough, and I was surprised.

"Isn't he the one who teaches here?" I heard myself wanting to start something and I couldn't control it. I was worried about what she was thinking because she wasn't giving me the whole story, I believed.

She ignored my question. "I would have told you if I had had something to tell you, but I wasn't sure of anything. I hadn't planned to keep anything from you."

"Well, I don't get it," I said.

"I don't either. Now sit with me while I do the ironing. Let me hear about you."

That was it? I wondered.

There was no way I was going to talk about me. I followed her into their bedroom which I had only been in once or twice before. They usually kept the door closed. It was a big dark room with a dark wooden dresser that had a half-moon mirror on it, an exercise bicycle in one corner in front of a sliding closet. The ironing board was on the other side of the bed, in front of a window that looked out over the endless green Winston fields. Terri turned the radio on, classical music as always, and she started taking clothes out of a round plastic basket on the floor. It was a little spooky with Shep gone. She was drinking her wine from a jelly glass that rested on the edge of the anvil-shaped board. She didn't seem to have any dread of picking up Shep's underwear and shirts along with everyone else's, even though he wasn't there any-more. She tipped the basket to make a pile on the floor where she could find things faster. She ironed and I was quiet. The room was quiet too, except for the little hisses as she dripped white wine from her fingertips onto the clothes before press-ing them. There hadn't been so many quiet times like this with Terri and it made me a little afraid. I assumed the si-lence wasn't my fault or her fault, it just was. Every few min-utes I'd hear a car horn or the shriek of a Winston student. I sat on the bed, my elbows on my knees, chin on my hands, watching her, watching her hands turn socks inside out, watching her curved back, worrying about what would hap-pen to us. She was humming to herself.

I was unprepared to see the tears on her face when she turned around. She walked toward me and sat down like a catcher between my knees, her hands balancing on the flat tops of her thighs. She put her glass down next to her. I was listening amazingly close, when she started, "I want you to kick me if . . . ," but what I heard was "kiss me," and her face was like a magnet and when I leaned down her lips were hot and kissing back. I saw how close her face was to mine and closed my eyes. I thought of the word "smooch" that Terri liked to use. I don't know how long we kissed, but when it was over I felt as red-faced as a kid waking from a nap.

Somehow, I had fallen off the bed and was sitting on the floor with her, our knees mixed together.

Then a noise came out of her chest, a laugh, low, a growl and a laugh, and she smiled as if to say "That was great," but she said, "Act your age." Then, "Go get me some more ice for my wine."

Although I was disappointed because I knew that was it, I was also happy and my lips were burning. I felt a little better seeing her like her old self. I took credit for it. At the freezer, I grabbed one cube in each hand and as I walked back I could feel them melting. She was still sitting on the floor and I dropped them in her jelly glass. She stood and hugged me, my face buried in the side of her neck. A friendly hug. I was nervous, shivering.

"No point worrying about times ahead," she said. "It'll be okay."

She was talking, but I wasn't really hearing. I knew from her tone that no more was ever going to happen between us. Now two things had happened that we were never really going to talk about, at least in the joking way we used to.

CHAPTER 20

Junior Goff overdosed. I heard during first period, the rest of the school heard at noon, a lot of kids gagging on their lunches in the cafeteria, the guys at the white door having a good laugh, and we all had the first Friday afternoon off in May, starting at 2:00. The funeral was scheduled for the next day.

I had never seen Billy so shaken. I got a call from the principal's office during math. Some girl, who hoped to get into college by working alongside the principal on Friday mornings, came to the classroom door, inched it opened and signaled for Mr. Volpo to leave his seat in the back where he usually sat while letting Dakin and some of the geniuses work the board. Worse than interrupting Mr. Volpo during lunch was interrupting him during this class. It was his easiest class and it brought him the greatest rewards, the math team acing out the rest of New Jersey year after year, a kind of deluxe basketball team in highwaters. Volpo figured the girl was there to deliver some bureaucratic bad news (I could tell he hated the administrators), but when she asked for me to be excused to go to the principal's office he seemed mildly entertained. He wished me good luck on the way out and told me to "come clean." He also winked.

I asked my messenger what was up, but she wouldn't turn back to look at me.

I saw Billy through the glass of Mr. Delaney's door, some other guys from the basketball team, Bobo and Sant, and a few black faces I knew from the black door. They were standing around Mr. Delaney like some huddle. Delaney was the shortest.

"Glad they found you, Will," Mr. Delaney said.

"Math. You know," I said. I had met Delaney only once, when at the end of a term it turned out I had missed over half my Spanish classes (I swore that it was just a strange accident) and Mrs. Renriga wanted to expel me. I was getting an A at the time, which was difficult to explain unless you knew the other Spanish students I was in with.

Billy was looking at me with no good humor and the others were looking down, unhappy about being this near Delaney I figured.

"Your friend from the basketball team, Julius Goff, expired last night," Delaney said, straight-faced. A few eyes looked up at me to see what I'd do with this news, but after I determined that expired meant dead, all I said was "How?"

"He choked on a chicken bone. He died quickly, before they could get him to breathe again."

I checked out Billy's face and it didn't budge.

"The funeral is tomorrow," Delany said, "and these boys thought that since you and Goff got on so well, you should be one of the pallbearers."

Bobo said, "You, me, Billy, Sant, Threets, and Sweeney."

"You should stay in this office for the rest of the day, which will end early," Delaney went on, "so that after I make an announcement you will be here to look after any students who come in with questions or just want to talk." Delaney didn't seem upset and was in a hurry to leave. He had other work to do and did not want to be around. He was probably glad Junior didn't die on school property.

When Delaney had stopped huffing, I took Billy's wrist and dragged him outside.

"What did he take?" I asked.

"Dust, I think," Billy said. "Went crazy. Went out for fast food and blew away like a door getting opened too hard."

"No chicken bones."

"What did you expect?" Billy said.

I wondered for a second if Billy knew more about Goff and his OD and wasn't telling me. Then my mind moved to the more extreme idea that Billy himself was a drug addict. That my best friend was in on a drug ring, making money on the side. Then I stopped such television thinking and I looked at him again and he gave it back to me and we were fine.

I didn't have a suit. I wore gray pants and a blue jacket. I drove across town to the Third Baptist Congregation and about half the school was there, the half that was black and about six and a half white people. I also saw some teachers. They stood around talking with each other, not paying any attention to kids they didn't want to see on a day off. The church was tiny, ivy covered, with birds' nests along the gutters and a big red door with a big bronze handle. In the room outside the sanctuary, they had Goff. He had probably never been in a church before.

There was a line formed to get to him. He was in an airless little room with two doors and a chair in front of the coffin which was up on a table about chest high. The room was thickly carpeted with drape-covered walls. In order, one at a time, people went up to the coffin and had a word with Junior, the rest of the line watching. I jumped in without much trouble, a few of my teammates pushing me forward, mumbling, "Pallbearer."

Goff looked like a fancy chocolate in a gift box. He was sunk in crushed red velvet. He had a better suit than mine and his little mustache seemed dusted. There was no mystery about him and when I got up there I waited for him to smile, faked like I had something to say to him, and let it go at that, letting the others through. I had liked him because he was the only player on the team smaller than I was, but he whined and regularly had bloody lips from driving inside without forethought of elbows. He was also dumb as a toaster oven. I never *saw* him use drugs, but I heard what everyone else did. Billy always had to shoo him away from his girls when he was high.

The ceremony had wailing and demands for freedom and constant shouts of amen! but nothing really changed the fact that Goff had screwed up. There were "Praise the Lords" and tambourines banged on open palms. They were all crying over the tragedy of a chicken bone. That was still the line a day later. I was listening to the hollering and thinking about Terri. I thought about Goff and Terri and how it is when you try to understand something you don't understand. I remembered Terri's stories about her friends, stories that were largely pointless about marriages and money and illnesses. But they were stories that never bored me, that I still

141

had questions about, questions she would have tried to answer while she was methodically cutting lettuce or dealing me seven gin rummy cards, throwing them at me like Frisbees.

I thought of calling Terri and telling her how confused I was by nearly everything. She should stay with the life she had chosen, stay with Shep and Clare and Kenny and Gina, not harm them. I would tell her how we had moved when I was ten years old, from a house where we had lived happily and unhappily, and then the house was empty, just scuffed and faded paint. I wondered for years who lived there next, in that emptiness. But I knew I would not call her and that if I saw her again I would be unable to say any of those things when she gave me a friendly smile. I felt sick and angry and I knew that I was crying.

I sat next to Billy who looked concerned. His ears twitched when he was nervous. I wondered who would have showed up if it were me up there, not Junior. My math class. Billy. Sara with her boyfriend. No one would let Terri know because my mother wouldn't have the address.

I tried to think about my father's funeral during the service. My father was perfectly clear to me, but I couldn't recall a thing about his funeral, who was there, who spoke, who I sat next to. Then I thought of what I remembered best of my father: the odd, bland foods he cooked and the color of the feather in his hat brim, but not a thing about his funeral came back to me.

Billy had explained to me the duties of pallbearing after asking his mother, who was there in a plum dress and a peaked black hat. After the service, we went up front and hefted the big thing with its cool bronze handles. I kept thinking that Goff wasn't that big, as we led the crowd out into the glare.

I got more than a few funny looks carrying the coffin. They came mostly from mean-looking black guys about 30 years old, people who I'd never seen in my life. Their eyes said nothing; they just studied me. I couldn't figure them out. Then near the exit, I got one annoyed look, and soon after a really angry one. Goff was heavy on my shoulder. I heard someone whisper viciously, "Who's he?" and my neck sank down into my shoulder as I tried to hurry forward.

We finally juggled him into the hearse. I gestured goodbye to Goff and when I turned around I felt like there was a crowd staring at me. I got nervous suddenly. Then a hand grabbed my elbow. It was Cerise.

"The few people who might have cared about him think there shouldn't be a whitey carrying his coffin," she said into my ear.

I looked at her in disbelief. And what was Cerise doing with the word "whitey"? She had on a black suit and a small black hat.

"What do you know?" I said, losing control. But I had the feeling she knew plenty.

"I'm his cousin," she said.

I stared at her and knew she was not lying.

"I don't want to pressure you or worry you," she said, "but I think you've done your work. If you go to the cemetery, give things a little distance."

I had never felt in danger before, or felt I was in the wrong part of town, like some of my classmates complained about. But I knew she was right. I found Billy and asked him to drive me to the cemetery. I didn't tell him about Cerise, but I was a little shaky.

I heard planes passing overhead and I could watch them a long way out there, in the open, among the white stones. They hadn't even gotten around to planting grass in the area that Goff got put in. I stood outside the grave circle making foot prints and thinking back to what happened outside the church. I realized that I was a white guy carrying a coffin. The praise I had been expecting for my good deed would never come. I thought for the first time about how my friends on the team always whispered when they were talking about white people. I don't mean when they were talking about *me*, but about white people in general. Something in them made them whisper. But none of those black guys was whispering outside that church when they saw me. They were giving me that "Fuck this shit, back your ass up," sort of look in loud eye shouts. I was cut off, just like that. I wasn't a different sort of white guy to them, just the other camp. Angry, feeling my sarcasm coming on, there was nothing I could do or say without ending up like Goff. I was lucky Cerise came over.

* * *

After all I'd been through with Sara in the few good days after our first big kiss, the sneaking of other kisses and more when Gary wasn't around, the trickery, my good intentions, my bad intentions, the on-the-bed scuffles among her stuffed animals, all our talk about what was "phony," and about getting rich and what diseases we might die from, and then the weekend at the Sidelys' dragging her back toward my love by bringing up my dead father for sympathy, after all that, she still had another boyfriend.

I hadn't really spoken with her much in the weeks since the weekend at the Sidelys'. She had taken away from that weekend an uncertainty about me. She was still a knockout, and once when I tried again to express my admiration in the school halls (we no longer walked to school together), she got upset. She said I was lying. She said, "Do something about it," like some bully. I began to avoid her and also the choices I had to make about her.

The day I got pulled out of Volpo's, the geniuses were discussing randomness. In particular, the art of estimation, the idea of expected value. I led the class and the power of probability lit up our little room for fifty minutes. The geniuses may not have taken it personally but I did, and by the end, I saw probabilities ricocheting through my recent life. I began to think that giving due weight to chance was a sign of growing up, and I thought of Sara.

I called her when I got home from Goff's funeral and said, "Let's go into the city to a museum tomorrow."

You can fool yourself about yourself, but Sara couldn't fool me. Despite the suspicions on the other end of the phone, I knew she was not going to refuse, whatever other plans she had already. Love does not have to be about going public, but I couldn't hoodwink her anymore by acting distracted. What she wanted was a public display of affection, even if it were in New York City where we weren't going to see anyone we knew. Something in me had tipped over.

"Why should I?" she asked. A good question.

"As a favor to me?"

"As long as you understand that, it's a deal."

"That's good." But I didn't know if it was that good because of the way my stomach lifted under my ribs.

I had the bus routes picked out so I would impress her with my knowledge of public transportation, a city regular. It took two connections. Billy's mom worked for Mass Transit so I had it made. Although one of my goals in life was to drive my own car into New York City just to cut off a yellow cab, then to drive home in triumph, I decided to spare Sara this dream.

It was a show of Picasso drawings. I explained to her when we got there that I would "donate" her admission fee (which meant "pay up" in any other than the fake language they used on museum signs), and we were in.

I had done some reading about Picasso. I gave her the basics: where he was born, when he died, where he lived.

Sara said, "Oo-la-la, a regular tour guide."

The goal of the day was to impress her. From there I figured it wouldn't be far for her to fall completely in love with me all over again. I told her that as an old man Picasso had had young wives. I told her his line about, "It's not what the artist does that counts but what he is," seeing some connection when I read it between that line and my relation with her.

"So now you're an intellectual."

"I just look."

Her eyes widened in mock terror.

We stopped at drawings from 1907 to 1914. We walked very slowly, holding hands. Sara would squeeze and sneak her fingers up my wrist, and when we walked between galleries I put my arm around her shoulder, releasing her when we entered the next room so that she could get close to a particular picture. For all my talk, the drawings bored me. They were childish. I stood back and considered Sara's poses as she studied the lines. She had on a black skirt over black woolen tights. Her frizzed hair was black over her olive sweater. She was soft and round while the art was not: a reed pipe, a broken bottle, a tipped glass.

About halfway through, Sara asked, "How did he stay so young?"

"He was just restless," I said, trying to sound mature.

"I think he's a genius," she said.

"He thought the same."

"Don't be so critical. Next you'll be critical of me."

"I don't think so."

I enjoyed our private time, the quiet of the museum, the skylights, and the cool draft of the air-conditioning about neck level. Sara moved ahead of me and I admired her ankles and the pull of her shirt over her hips. I lost sight of her going into the last room as I stopped to look at a fruit dish, and when I turned the corner she popped out and said, "Step into my lips," this kiss ending after about a minute.

When I pulled back, I saw over her shoulder a familiar head of hair across the gallery, hurrying out past the last partition. Each strand was in place and it was gray. My eyes caught the man's back and I knew the angle of his midsection overhanging his belt. Then my eyes leaped to the curl of his arm guiding the small of a woman's back, a woman in a lime green suede jacket. I saw him lean toward her and kiss her mouth. Then the two of them were gone behind a partition.

I continued to look at the drawings but I walked fast, directly across the gallery in the direction of this mirage. I forgot about Sara. When I got to the exit, there was Lester, alone, approaching me.

"I thought that was you in the middle of that kiss," he said, cheerily.

There was no one with him.

"That's me, kissing," I said.

"Did you like the show?"

"How could I?" I said. My forearms felt tight, my hands were opening and closing.

"Listen. I'd like to meet your friend, but my meter's running out," he said, showing me a quarter he had just taken from his pocket. "So I'll probably see you this week." He shook my hand.

I couldn't say anything else, but my heart was jumping and my fists were clenching again.

Sara found me as Lester was walking away.

"A friend of yours?"

"You never know who you'll see." I was shaking my head. "A friend of my mother's."

Sara had already hooked arms with me and was walking me out of the museum into the too-bright city street.

My mother didn't own any green coats; she hated green.

It is really difficult to prove what you believe. I was certain that it was Lester I'd seen in the museum. After all, he shook my hand and talked to me. When he came up to me he was alone, so I wasn't absolutely sure that he had been with another person. Well, yes I was. But I wasn't exactly sure that the other person had been a woman. Well, yes I was. But who was to say that Lester was touching her in any romantic way. Maybe it was his aunt or his sister.

Sometimes you can't know things with certainty. I didn't know, for instance, that I could keep Sara happy for an afternoon on a real date. However by midweek, in the sullen, dead-Goff atmosphere of school, I had reviewed every detail of that afternoon with her as if it were my first date, which in some sense, it was. I remembered playing with the top button of her shirt as we rode the bus home, just absentmindedly flicking it in and out of its hole while we talked. I remembered how private it felt inside, with the roar of the bus all around us, just loud enough to cover all sounds but our voices. The seat backs were high and no one was across from us; we were alone. She asked lots of questions about my parents. I ended up telling her things that probably made me look like the suffering side of a bad mother-son gag.

I told her about my mother coming up behind me just that week when I was doing the dishes, which I've done every night that I've been home since my father died, and throwing her arms around me and hugging me tight. Her chubby arms made a lock around my chest.

"It was horrifying," I told Sara.

But she had no understanding of this horror. She asked me, "Why?"

"Because it was." Which was no way of explaining how this chest-lock was just my mother's way of being needy and I didn't want to be the needed. It wasn't my job. When she did stuff like that it reminded me of my father. She should have been giving him the chest-lock and leaving me alone.

"And when I picked her fingers off, one by one," I told

Sara, "my mother just stood behind me hovering. Watching me put dish soap on my sponge and run it around a plate for about five minutes. Until I shouted at her, 'Move!'"

Sara looked at me as if I were an ax murderer, and I wondered why I was ruining a perfectly good time with such stories. When a son gets asked about his mother he should say only, "I don't have a mother. An aunt gave birth to me," or something else silly and evasive.

Our date wound down in this odd way of me telling mean stories which I learned never to repeat. It ended with plenty of fun too, another long kiss.

I suppose I started telling Sara my needy mother stories because I wanted my mother to need Lester rather than me. Now I wasn't sure about Lester after what I'd seen at the museum.

I explained none of my Lester doubts to Sara. The bigger problem was whether to tell any of it to my mother.

CHAPTER 21

Whether to tell my mother what I knew, was a dilemma that had no single answer. What I knew about her and chose not to tell her was, of course, my great advantage over her in a life that had its troubles. The mothers I'd met believed basically that their children were not paying attention to them. They complained about this often to their friends. Or at least my mother did. How many times had I heard her say, "He's in his own world" when really I was just acting bored in order to take it all in. She told her friends that I did not call her when I said that I would, or, that I'd made plans when she and I already had plans. She told them that if I was, in fact, paying attention to her, then I did not have a very good memory because all the things I did to upset her I did over and over again. Basically, she told her friends that I was uncaring. My mother believed that she could relate to me through a one-way mirror; she could see me, but I could not see her. How wrong.

There must be a million mother-son gags. I knew that in some places, like the black door for instance, jokes about mothers made people mad. This started in elementary school, but the retaliation grew fierce right into adulthood. I heard boxers saying "Your momma" to each other in the ring when Wide World of Sports dropped that mike right into the middle of them during the late rounds of big fights. I heard it at school, at my shoe store, in the movies. "Playing the dozens," as Billy clued me. None of it bothered me though. The defense of my mother was not a priority.

Which led right up to this question: did I have to like someone I was related to? I had always assumed that I liked her. When she was with my father, he seemed happy enough. And he saw her peskiness, her stunts, and her unsteady moods up close. He had a sense of humor about her, although he had to escape into the basement with his math books when she was too much. He was able to recover enough to grade papers and help me with homework and not blink at his plight. I never thought much about me and my mother specifically until he died. Then there we were, just the two of us. I had less of a sense of humor than my father did.

When he died, all the widows of the street brought over food and we went into a trance for a week. After that, my mother was unnaturally sane for about three weeks, which I should have seen as a bad sign. She never said, "What did I do to deserve this?" but I was sure she was thinking it. I figured that she would first be laid flat like she had had an illness and then she would rebound optimistically, thankful for my help. But her convalescence was actually one long selfish mood that continued for years—really until she met Mr. Lester Warner. A television too loud or a spill on the counter set her off. She didn't have enough attention to sit and sort photos or read, but she was always ready to be bossy toward me. I had taken over her chores, the ironing and cooking and dishes and vacuuming, and she got used to that routine, so when she began to work again she never took her chores back. The dishes were fine because there's nothing more relaxing than warm water, but I hated cleaning the refrigerator.

Knowing something about Lester Warner that she didn't know seemed a great luxury but also a pain. I went to school the week after our museum meeting dreading his next visit. Luckily there were distractions at Bergenville High. On the afternoon of the school costume party, some clown threw a lead pipe into Mr. Delaney's office. Actually into the room outside his, where a secretary usually sat, but Delaney happened to be typing his own letter and took it on the rear of the skull and his upper shoulder with a lot of blood and blanching according to those who answered his scream. He walked around with a turban and if you stood behind him you could see that his ear had turned marine green mixed with yellow. It had probably been a simple prank, aimed at no one in particular and just heaved over a shoulder, but Delaney took it personally. He sent his senior (hoping to get into college) spies out to listen for rumors. You could see them standing just outside the small groups of students that formed in the hallways between classes. The spies would pretend like they had misplaced something in a notebook and lean in with their ears.

I knew who did it. Some of the real brain-children from the white door were crossing in front of the school after hours, around four P.M., when they passed Dakin in their getups: motorcycle club outfits, Charles Manson masks. They were a little afraid of Dakin because he was strong-looking and fearless, but they also despised him because he was smart. Dakin wanted everyone to like him, so when he passed them he admired their outfits. A couple of them were carrying lead pipes as any decent Hell's Angels would and they challenged him to a contest of who could throw the heavy pipes highest into the air. Delaney got hit when someone pushed Dakin during his turn, sending the pipe hurtling off toward the school. Dakin told me the story and I had to spend all of one lunch explaining to him why he shouldn't turn himself in.

His regret and bad feeling continued right into the weekend when he rang my doorbell at about 8 A.M. Saturday.

"Forget about it," I said. I decided to let him in.

"Those guys pushed me," he said.

"I have no doubt," I told him. "But Delaney will."

I had never seen Dakin confused before. He kept moving around the kitchen, fixing me with worried looks.

"Here's what you should do," I said. It had taken me days to come up with a good idea. "Go back to the spot where the pipe left your hand, take a few measurements, draw a few vectors and calculate its speed when it reached the school. If you feel confident in your numbers then we'll tell Delaney. If not, we drop the charges once and for all."

Turning it into a math problem was, I must admit, a stroke of genius on my part. But that's how it worked with Dakin. I knew the answer would be slippery and he could stop bothering me. He asked if he could borrow a pencil and an index card and he left without another word.

Lester Warner arrived about ten minutes after Dakin left. I wished that I had made plans for the weekend, that I had left with Dakin. Lester had a date with my mother, and he came in with his courting smile and a hand shake for me. My mother came down blinking like a chronic flirt and I had to leave the room in order to stop shuddering.

I could hear the two of them discussing the day: should they go to the zoo or to the city, where to eat lunch, a picnic perhaps (which meant having to stop at the market), or should they go to the Audubon Sanctuary and look for birds, and eat back here. I thanked God that Sara and I avoided those discussions by going to either her place or mine exclusively. The one time we went out I had landed information about Lester's interest in art that I now could not get rid of. I would have asked Terri for her advice, but I had no Terri to ask anymore.

When my mother came upstairs to change clothes, I went downstairs to avoid her.

"You want to join us on our bird walk?" Lester asked.

I had been on one birdwalk in my life, with my parents on Cape Cod. It had been hot and buggy, and all the adults (I was the only child dragged along) were wearing binoculars and looking upward. The guide told everyone to whisper if they saw something or heard something, and to walk quietly. I faded to the back of the pack, out of sight of the last woman who was strapped up with boxes and bags of bird books and camera equipment. From there, I made a variety of bird noises at a variety of angles. I had the whole line of them going crazy looking for the unseen tweeters they were sure had surrounded them. Even the guide was confused.

I looked at Lester, straight on, and said, "Absolutely not." Something inside stopped me from saying, "No fucking way." Then I said to him, "What should I tell her?"

"About what?" he asked, innocent.

"About our meeting in the museum."

"You haven't told her that you saw me?" he asked quietly. I saw that he had on tasseled shoes and wondered how they would do on the bird walk.

"Oh yes, of course. Mother dear, I saw your friend Lester and his date at the Museum of Modern Art last weekend."

"My date?" Now he was pushing it.

"I'm sorry," I said, getting sarcastic, "is there another word for it at your age?"

He just looked at me, his head tipped about five degrees, his hair not moving a millimeter.

"Excuse me. You were with a woman there, weren't you?"

Now he looked at me carefully, but he didn't pause. I could tell though that he was surprised I had seen her. The meter routine had probably worked before.

"Well, what should I tell my mother?"

"Tell her the truth," he said.

I was not expecting it, and that answer was like a speedy punch before I could get into a crouch. I felt unsure, pounded. I wanted to grab him on my way down to the canvas.

I heard a bell go off, one rattling ding, and I went over to get my egg from the water, soft-boiled.

CHAPTER 22

I wanted to speak with Terri, to tell her all this news and get her line on it, but I was afraid to speak with her. The more I thought about it, the more I thought that things had ended between us, and ended badly.

I called on a Thursday at around 8 P.M. when I figured she would be putting the kids to bed. After three rings, I heard a female voice answer, "Hello?"

I thought it sounded like Terri. "Terri? Is that you?" I ventured.

"This is Clare," Clare said.

"Clare, this is Will."

There was silence.

"Clare, this is Will. How are you?"

"My father's not home," she said.

"How are Kenny and Gina?"

"He'll be back later. He's at a meeting." Who was she kidding? I knew she was lying.

It finally clicked that she wasn't going to give me much. I knew we had never been pals but I never thought that we were enemies.

"At nine you say, huh."

"Right. Bye."

When I heard the dial tone I had the urge to call her back and give her a yelling like Terri would have after that behavior. Then I began to think about it and I thought maybe I should call her back and straighten things out between us, tell her I'd been abandoned too and go into the parallels. But the whole business seemed too complicated and horrible. I realized that I didn't want to talk to her and I didn't want Terri much either. I didn't really have anything to say. If Terri wanted to see me again, she would find me. And if she didn't, she wouldn't.

* * *

Mr. Volpo asked me to stay after class that Friday afternoon. Math was last period for me and I'd been looking forward to freedom and Sara. He closed the door and walked behind his desk. I was about six feet from him, at my desk, in the front row.

"Is Dakin the smartest kid you know?" he asked me.

"Yes," I admitted.

"Is Dakin the stupidest kid you know?"

"Yes."

"So what are we left with?"

I didn't know where he was going with this so I kept quiet.

"We're left with a stupid genius who throws lead pipes through windows."

I looked at him suspiciously. Was this a trap?

"You're wondering how I know that Dakin threw it," he said.

Actually, I was wondering who else on the teacher end of things knew. And when Delaney would be kicking Dakin out. I felt responsible somehow for Dakin, maybe because my father had.

I remembered my first meeting Dakin after a baseball game in the playground across from our house when he was carried over with a very bloody knee after a late slide into a home plate that was really just a collection of gravel. My father was the adult closest to the scene and he gave Dakin a good patching up which led to the two of them talking about math. They were pals after that, Dakin visiting my house sometimes just to see my father. His father was in the diamond business and knew only the grossest kind of mathematics.

"All sorts of tidbits come to my attention," Volpo said. "I've been around here long enough."

I let him keep talking.

"So what do you think we should do?" he asked me. "Who should we tell?"

"We?" I hadn't even agreed that it was Dakin with the lousy aim.

"To think about this and some other things, I'd like to invite you to my house now for a soda."

"That's very kind but . . . "

"Well then, let's go," he said, and was halfway to the door

even with his limp before I stood up. What was I going to say? He was showing me he was a regular guy underneath his gruffness.

Because school was officially over, only delinquents (kept after as punishment) and goody-goodies (hanging around to ask about extra credit) were in the hallways as we headed out. Mr. Volpo walked slowly because of his limp, so rather than getting embarrassed about being seen with him in our coats, I faced down anyone who dared to look at us with a stare that said, "You'll never know the importance of what Mr. Volpo and I are about to do. Never." I followed him to the teacher's parking lot and we got into his little Mazda.

We drove about ten minutes, just past one of our town's shopping areas—one long block of pharmacies, ice cream shops, a toy store, a deli, two record stores, a jewelry place— to where his apartment building was located, surrounded by large trees. It was warm for early May. We parked on the side and rode the elevator to the third floor, all the while talking about my other classes and next year's basketball team outlook. I had never told him that I played basketball.

He rang the bell and opened the door with his key at the same time. A small Filipino woman appeared, shy, and pretty in a blue skirt.

"This is my wife, Manya," he said, and she nodded but didn't speak, backing up. I felt embarrassed for her but had no reason to; she was probably very happy. He didn't introduce me to her but led me to this tiny living room which had a big stereo system on an empty bookcase, two stumpy couches at right angles with low wooden stools in front of them on a throw rug. There was a photograph of an atomic blast on one wall, and the other walls were empty. He left me sitting there alone.

When he came back he was in shorts and I could see the knee that didn't bend, the one that I always wondered about in class. It had a pink scar facing the other knee. His calves were thin. For the first time, I was really unhappy to be there.

"Soda?" he offered. But I had given up soda because of the rotten-teeth risks and just asked for water with ice.

Most older men ignored me even after they learned that I was fatherless. I'm talking about my school friends' fathers who, I could tell, felt that they never had enough time for themselves, let alone their wives and their own kids. They might give me a pat on the back, but they never asked me questions, preferring me as a stranger.

Volpo, I could now tell, was the opposite and that was the purpose of this visit. I'd seen this type of overboard friendliness once before in a basketball coach of mine whose kid was a spaz. He wanted me to replace his kid, I mean he wanted me to *be* his kid, so he could take credit for me. It was shaping up—Volpo's home, even his ice water—that he had no kids of his own.

He sat down on the other couch, his left leg out in front of me on its stool, his scar paler without the weight on it. I had all my school clothes on and he suddenly looked sloppy.

"I'm planning to retire," he said. "Did you know that?"

"No."

"I'm not reaching the students anymore." He took a long breath.

"That's not true in our class," I said.

"I get mad when I see kids like Dakin. This idiotic behavior of his. He should be getting serious."

I sipped my drink. I wasn't going to confirm the Dakin-pipe connection. When I took a deep breath, I realized the whole place smelled of cat food.

"I was good at math. Real good," he told me. "I worked hard. Then the war started and I'm in the Philippines and then I'm back and goddammit I'm not as good as I remembered I was. Or thought I was. After a few graduate courses, I see that people are better than I am. And I've married Manya, I need a paycheck, so I start teaching high school."

I saw that he had me all wrong. Mr. Volpo wanted to be my friend so that I could be his son, or some childless man's equivalent.

"You're great at math," I said.

"You'll see," he said.

I was about to ask him what this had to do with Dakin, but I restrained myself.

"You want to help me make questions for the next test?" he asked me. "Look, you always do well, what's the point in taking another test. Let's make a hard one for the others and that will be your test, coming up with the questions."

At first I thought I hadn't heard him right. Then I knew what he was after, and I saw myself skipping the test, and one of the others—probably Dakin—noticing that I never made it up. I saw Mr. Volpo was trying hard to be my friend and it didn't seem right. He must have seen me as the only near-normal one in the class, the only one he had a shot at capturing.

"I don't think that I can be of much help."

"Sure. Okay," he said. He took off his glasses and wiped them.

His eyes also seemed to clear.

"Now as for Dakin," he said. "I want you to know that he's never going turn into anything good if he keeps it up."

I should have just ridden it out, but I said, "Don't bet against Dakin."

He looked at me as if I had missed the lesson he was trying to give me in his living room. He seemed disgusted.

"Finish up that water," he said in the old voice I recognized, and while I gulped, he picked up his wallet and keys.

He decided to let me off back at school, possibly to pretend he was beginning again, that this visit had never happened. As we drove, I thought of a newspaper article I had recently finished, about old people in Florida starting a crime wave. Seventy-year-olds shoplifting all over Miami. They didn't need the perfume and wallets they stole, it was obvious. They only wanted attention and I imagined Mr. Volpo one of them, being dragged down to police headquarters to get lectured. I heard him saying to the police sergeant the same thing one of the Florida men said: "What about getting old, and not having what you want? Shouldn't different laws apply?"

CHAPTER 23

After Volpo suggested that I create a test for my classmates, I spent a week sorting through a red leather suitcase filled with my father's old papers, looking at some tests that he gave in his probability classes. I found one that I liked, but I never gave it to Mr. Volpo.

I knew that the geniuses would not be tripped up easily. Most people in my school believed, for instance, that when a newscaster said there was a 50% chance of rain on Saturday and a 50% chance of rain on Sunday, that there was a 100% chance of it raining over the weekend, and that all beach plans should be cancelled. The geniuses would only laugh at such pathetic thinking.

This was the problem:

Suppose you were a person who discovered, while doodling with some chemicals in your kitchen, what you thought might be a new sexual lure for mosquitos. This idea came to you because many mosquitos seemed to have wandered over to where you were madly mixing your liquid supplies. But you could not be sure that these mosquitos weren't merely lost, or looking for a place to spend a few moments of a sunny summer afternoon, or just buzzing over to you by chance. You needed a way to prove, or at least become a little bit surer, that you had stumbled onto a mosquito love potion. So you devised an experiment.

You bought a small Y-shaped glass tube that had openings at its three ends. You stoppered the two prongs of the Y with cotton, one cotton soaked with water, the other soaked with your discovery. Then you went down to the local pond and captured exactly twenty mosquitos in a jar. You attached this jar to the bottom end of the Y-shaped tube with a funnel, allowing the mosquitos to go down the short straightaway of the tube toward the two arms, and the two soaked cottons.

Let's assume that the mosquitos went freely following their own mosquito desires, that they were not bumped off course by other mosquitos, that they did not follow some bully leader mosquito. Each one went where it wanted to go.

If 17 turned toward your newly discovered love potion, did the experiment indicate that your substance was enticing them?

Solution:

Well, if your supposed potion was really no more of an attractant than water, we'd expect, on average, ten of the twenty mosquitos to have proceeded toward it, and the other ten to have turned toward the cotton soaked with water. Just like if we flipped a coin, there would be a 50% probability it would come up tails. If you flipped that coin a couple of times, betting on tails, and it kept coming up heads, and you trusted the coin and its owner, you'd say it was just a matter of bad luck. If half of the mosquitos went each way, we'd say, yeah that's what we expected. But let's say that 11 went one way and 9 went the other way, how sure would we be that that was a simple coincidence? If 12 flew one way and 8 flew the other way, would that be just a funny luck of the draw? How about 13 and 7? In our experiment, 17 flew one way and 3 flew the other way. Wasn't that evidence that more than luck was at work, that your discovery really was a sexy substance?

When I gave it to my classmates informally, the geniuses got it right, every one of them. Was *that* just a matter of luck? I'd say not: they all knew the binomial distribution. They set up the following formula $\sum_{X=17}^{20} \binom{20}{x}(\frac{1}{2})^X(\frac{1}{2})^{20-X}$ and came up with the answer that there was a probability of 0.1% (about one in a thousand chance) that seventeen mosquitos would fly one way and three the other by sheer coincidence. Our kitchen chemist had in all likelihood discovered a new sex trap.

It was of course possible (one in a thousand) that the mosquitos had gone the way they had merely by coincidence. But that was pretty unlikely. Not impossible however. Just pretty damn unlikely. Perhaps a little more likely than a tourist getting killed by a terrorist while on vacation. Neither was impossible though.

If Sara agreed to go out with me seventeen out of twenty times, well now, *that* was impossible.

CHAPTER 24

I still had the truth sitting on top of me. How to handle the truth was the greatest uncertainty in a life of probabilities. So I headed the two blocks over to Sara's. It was nippier than I thought and when I rang her doorbell my legs had gooseflesh. I don't know why I was surprised to see her at 9:30 A.M. on a Saturday morning in a nightgown but I was. I had never seen her in one before.

"Hi. Have you had breakfast yet?" she asked, as if she were expecting me.

"I should have brought my egg," I said.

I could see her ankles as I followed her into the kitchen and when I got up on a stool beside the counter next to the stove and watched her move and bend below me I could see down on the top of her breasts. Her nightgown was white with vertical red stripes and lace trim on the neck and hem. It made her body look long.

"Isn't a true family supposed to be eating breakfast together on a weekend?" I asked.

"My parents are out walking," she said. I suddenly felt it getting big in my pants. I also felt nervous for no good reason that I could think of.

"My mother and Lester are about to bird walk themselves." A new weekend, a new bird walk.

"Who's Lester?"

I realized that after many months of Lester Warner I hadn't said a thing about him to Sara.

"Remember the guy I met in the museum? That's Lester."

"You never told me his name." And I had never told my mother Sara's name.

"I could tell you a lot more about him now. Not much of it good."

Seeing Sara had immediately returned me to a good mood and I didn't feel like slipping back.

162

Sara finished putting apricot jelly on some bread and came to sit on the stool next to mine. The seats were wicker and our butts sank in while our knees came up.

I said, "You know, I tried to sculpt a knee once in art class in fifth grade and I failed miserably." I put my hand on her knee and meandered around with my fingers. I thought of Billy's fingers.

Then before I could put the sweet toast between my teeth, she had leaned over and kissed me on the mouth and eyes and forehead and chin. I could feel her loose breasts against me. I thought of how Sara was always giving me things. The smallest gifts had seemed so generous—a funny card, a plastic watch with the President's face, a tiny pewter animal that looked like a kangaroo, a Three Stooges mug. How I had unwrapped the package she handed me on her version of my sixteenth birthday and found a hopping penis toy that you could wind up and have it jerk around a table top. And I realized finally what that present had meant and how ignorant I'd been of its too obvious message.

Her hand went to one of my knees and up and up and undid my belt, then down and down and snapped the elastic edge of my underwear on its way south. It was unexpected like everything else that morning, but I felt nervous and lucky. She was being generous again.

"When are your parents coming back?"

But she already had my hand and was leading me upstairs. I said, "Doesn't this usually happen on a park bench, or a parked car or a rooftop?" I was nervous even behind my knees.

When we got into her room I put her hand back onto the bulge in my pants giving her the funny little man with his army helmet. It was fun watching her undress in the broad light, even with her back to me. My feet felt jumpy and I was thinking of what I'd tell Billy. What I'd seen. I'd say, "You won't believe what's under there . . ." Of course he knew all about it. She kept her earrings in that tan Indonesian basket. I felt freed up and I drew my own shirt off and lay back on her bed. I crossed my hands behind my head because they were trembling.

Sara walked toward me and all I could say was, "Is that you?" Then my mouth went dry and silent. I saw one of her knees on the bed and then her lowering herself and her breasts that seemed so light in my hands. My own knee rested against the bone over her pubic hair.

I said, "Before breakfast?"

She said, "You have other plans?"

My lower half was under attack, twisted and hot. She knew what to do next so I let her. I kept telling her how beautiful she was over and over again, so I wouldn't have to listen to my own heart pounding. I'm sure she could feel me shaking. Strands of her damp hair kept falling into my face. I was growling and panting and watching in foolishness and confusion. I felt crazy and told her so. I showed her things I meant to show her and looked for things I had thought about for a long time. There were some slow, achy moments, our eyes open with delight, but a lot of it was fast and impossible. She gripped everything, pumped it. I held her pretty, naked, happy body hard.

When we were half done I said to her, "I was the kind of little kid who put everything in his mouth." I didn't know what I was saying. It was spewing out of me. I didn't know what I was doing; I'd probably done half of it wrong.

She said, "Good."

I felt weak. The ceiling seemed low and crowded. I felt old and stupid for missing this before. My father would have said even at my ripe age of 16 I was within the bell curve.

If Terri were around and we got into a serious discussion about her first time I would have said, "I didn't expect to learn anything new," just to get her. I was glad Sara knew a lot.

Sara said at the end, "It's lucky God makes people horny when they're young and already insane."

I was wobbly when I tried to walk. I went back and checked her pulse. It was slow.

I was thinking: as we grow up and get smarter this will get even better.

CHAPTER 25

Gary was a goner. That's what I was thinking on the way home as I recalled the details of Sara. I knew that I would remember the heat and sounds forever and I was glad it had happened first in the morning sunshine. I remembered the movements of Sara's hand in her hair, one finger guiding loose strands over her right ear, the way her shoulder blade stuck out in back when her arm bent, and I knew that that was it for Gary no matter what he wanted from her.

Now I had to get rid of Lester for my mother. In my good mood I had decided to help her out.

When I got into the house, I called Sara. To thank her and for moral support.

When she answered, I told her, "I love you."

"I know that," she said. "Tell me some news."

"What's next with us?"

"More of the same."

"That's good to hear."

I had told her all about Lester while we were finishing the apricot toast.

"Now as for Lester," I said into the telephone.

"As a two-timer myself," she said, "I want you to go easy."

"That was in your past," I said. "See you in about an hour."

I wanted to go back to her house and start all over again.

My mother and Lester were at the kitchen table sipping coffee when I came in through the vestibule. They were talking investment strategies. Rather, he was giving her tips from his vast knowledge of both the stock market and chance. Maybe she was goofy enough to believe that she didn't know as much as he did. But if she went with her instincts, she was always right on the money. She simply bet on common thinking, what she knew. I had seen her holdings balloon. With Lester Warner however, she was docile.

As I went over in my mind what I would tell her about him, I tried to remember whether I'd ever seen her cry. She hadn't cried at my father's funeral, which I considered unbelievable and unforgivable. Or even the night he died on the bed next to her, his lungs filling up with fluid. I had seen her cry once when she fell with a bag of groceries on the rock-imbedded concrete of our driveway. The skin of her knee had folded back like a peach and the blood ran into the spilled brown paper bags. But that was a pain anyone would understand and she had been humiliated by her stumble.

Here was my nasty chance to get her to cry again.

I went right in, tapped her on the shoulder and said, "Can I speak with you?"

She gave me one of her looks that meant, This better be good. Her eyes were clear blue. The tiny red surface vessels on her cheeks gave her color. About a week before she met Lester Warner she had told me, "I'm fifty-five years old and I want to be happy every minute from now on." Which seemed a bit extravagant to me as a goal. But even during her extra time at work, I knew she was planning happy vacations, happy meals out, happy theatre dates for herself.

She got up from the table and followed me upstairs. I wanted her to hear this in my father's room, her room. When we got there, as if she had been reading my mind she said, "You know, I was thinking about your father today." I realized how rarely we spoke of my father and wondered how likely it was that this was due to chance. "And how different my life is now."

I heard Lester pounding around downstairs, scraping a chair across the floor, opening up the paper.

She sat down in a deep-back chair in the alcove a few feet from the end of the bed. I sat on the bed, on the edge, looking down on her a little in her sunken chair. She tried to make me look right at her, but I avoided her eyes.

"No one expects to fall in love when they're fifty-five," she said.

I was really avoiding eye contact now. I didn't want to encourage this line of conversation. I wanted to tell her about Mr. Lester Warner and then retreat.

"All my friends like Lester, you know?" I didn't know and didn't want to know.

"I'm lucky to have anyone at my age. I guess that comes right down to it. And he doesn't have any sexual hangups. He doesn't run around or drink and he cares for me."

That was enough. "How can you be with someone you don't love?" I was an expert now.

"He takes care of me."

"You're not helpless."

I couldn't make sense of her even though she'd lived with my father for thirty-two years. So I told her, "I can't figure this out."

"It's really very simple. There's nothing complicated about it."

"You'd rather have bad than none." I said it and thought immediately of Sara and Gary and me.

"It isn't bad. There are ups and downs. It might not seem so good because you grew up watching your father and me. Some things about your father I still miss. Talking about intellectual things instead of birds. But at least someone's listening when I say something. Look at my friends. They have nothing."

She almost had me crying. The conversation was not as I had planned.

"Your friends are nuts."

"Yes," she admitted, "but Lester spends time with me and basically cares for me whatever his faults. What bothers you about him?"

I had my shot, but I said, "Nothing."

"You know that if I met the perfect man and fell in love I would leave Lester in a minute."

I knew and she knew that there was no perfect man, or time like that again for her. Which really left me as the only one with good times to come. So I came to understand one basic law of probability that I had missed: we are prepared for the last thing that happened and not what's next.

CHAPTER 26

I got back to Sara's fast. Her parents were still out. We both knew what that meant and I went after her recently applied black bra, and with it gone, all the places on her bounced back. I was swirling around her, carrying on. I was now a pro. My tongue was rough and thick; parts of her seemed oiled. She had me undressed in no time once she had the idea, faster than I could have done it myself.

"Remember just a few weeks ago, you wouldn't say hello when I came near you, you wouldn't say goodbye when I left, and you wouldn't look at me when I was there?" she asked.

"No."

"I liked you about this much," she said, and gave my uncovered thing a twist.

"I surrender."

We played for a while until we heard that unmistakable parent-unlocking-the-front-door click.

Her cheeks were red from rubbing my cheeks and my cheeks were red from impure thoughts when we went down to see her parents. We had each put on powders to hide the other smells.

Her father said to me, "Will you're here early, huh."

"New hobby."

"You want breakfast?" he asked.

"I'm full."

"You're lucky in that. Sara," he said, "there are some dishes to do here."

"I gotta go now," I told her.

She gave me a pleasant enough look, filled with dislike for this dirty-dish abandonment, but I was glad for once that it was me doing the abandoning.

I touched her cheek then, in public, in front of her parents and I was proud and amazed. She was very correct walking me to the door, then gave me one of those birthday kisses as I headed out.

I had my car there, having wanted to save time that second visit. I thought again of calling Terri, but I felt it was cruel to slam her with good news. Instead, I drove directly to Billy's. It was near 11:00 and his mother let me in. We tiptoed to his room to wake him.

He looked peaceful just before I smacked my hand down on the sheet near his face. Billy's mouth puckered in disgust, then said, "This better be good." To cheer him up I went over to his tapedeck and switched it on. He only listened to black women singers whose names began and ended with the letter *a:* Anita, Aretha.

"I wouldn't trust me if I were you," I said.

"This better be good."

"You won't believe what's under there," I said. He must have had an inkling because he opened an eye.

"What's that?" he asked.

"Under her shirt and other places."

Then he woke up suddenly. "Not Sara," he said. "No."

"With abandon."

I wasn't planning to tell him anything specific because that was for me and Sara when he said, "Big deal," and lay back down. "Who else knows?"

"No one. I mean except I think her parents know."

Billy said, "The best part is not knowing anything one minute, then knowing *everything* the next. And how she looks at you when you know about her. How crazy it makes you." He had told me not long before that he was worried Linda was "straying," although he had no evidence to that effect.

Billy said, "What were the odds of a juvenile such as yourself getting a hot ticket like Sara?"

"I'm not sure," I answered.

"Ask the geniuses in math class," he said.

I drove back to Sara's house slowly, savoring all the heat on me trapped under my clothes. Sara gave me a lot of instruction as we walked over to my house so my mother could meet her. Sara had probably been storing up her ideas. For instance, she told me that I was the world's worst hand holder.

She grabbed my hand after telling me and said, "Put a little power into it." Then she explained restraint to me by asking me to hold her shirt down while she pulled her sweater over her head. I was not allowed to touch anything but her shirt. Those were important things. I was allowed to carry the sweater.

After she met my mother, Sara described her as "unsurprising and factual." When I asked her for about the eighth time if I should say something to my mother about Lester, she replied, "What you know, she doesn't want to know." It's funny how everyone who had the clearest picture of my mother barely knew her.

Sara told me that my mother loved me but had her own peculiar way of showing it. That all she knew was her sort of love. I told her that not all parents love their children, some are just mouths filling themselves.

"So why do I feel that I need her for more than food and shelter?" I asked Sara.

"Because she is the only one able to explain your father's past to you. She has that," Sara told me.

I could have tracked down my father's younger brothers in Charleston, South Carolina, and L.A. I knew that one designed submarines and the other was an astronomer at Cal tech. I could have found his statistics friends from the university where he'd taught for a few years. But all of them would have given me only the rosy view. What else would they tell some pathetic teenager showing up years later?

I believed that somewhere along the line I could depend on my mother. I've always believed that the truth could be determined if you knew how, and I was certain, certain like I was certain of nothing else, that I would be able to see through my mother's tricks, her turns from the truth when she spoke of my father. In the end, I would come up with some conclusions of my own.

CHAPTER 27

That very night, a Saturday, as I was watching the 11 o'clock news on my mother's bed (she was out with Lester), Terri called. She had never called me before so I had a second of disbelief when I heard her voice. Also I was a little distracted by the boxscores on TV.

She said, "Will, is that you?"

"Terri? Terri Kean of the Winston school?" I was making fun of her in a sweepstakes-winner announcement voice, but I was glad to hear her. "Terri, where are you?" I asked, all serious.

"I'm right here in New York City. A neighbor of yours." She sounded different.

"Before you go on, just tell me, are you going to see me anymore?"

"I hope I can see you tomorrow."

"Before I say yes or no, is Shep with you?"

"No he is not."

"Is that good or bad?"

"I'll tell you tomorrow," and she gave me the address of her hotel in Manhattan and a time to meet her.

I used my mother's car to drive into the city late on Sunday morning. Bergenville was still asleep. A few joggers were out, some cats were loafing, and there was some litter rolling down the street toward the highway. My hometown looked like a parade had passed through the day before. Which it hadn't. The sycamore trees, just budding, urged me into the past, to the small roads of Connecticut on my way to the Winston School, the cheap hotels and shacks with tin chimneys, the March cattails waving dry and brown, the empty picnic tables disappearing into a few trees. I thought of conversations I had had with Terri in her house with the babies in their rooms before Shep had left. Terri listening so closely to everything I said that she didn't hear the youngest crying. I remembered a conversation where I told her, "You have too many choices," when she complained of feeling stuck in Connecticut. "Never," she had answered. And I said, "You need dire necessity," which I had meant as a joke, only to hear her answer, "I need choices that wait for me." That had been the first time I had a glimpse that she was not as carefree as I'd imagined. I remembered my weekends at the Winston school as pure anticipation, as good as anything, as good as love can be.

Manhattan on the upper West Side was also asleep, but each block I walked from where I parked to her hotel smelled either of brewed coffee or of the ocean. I was looking forward to seeing Terri and was trying to stay calm. All the good moments with her came creeping over me.

She was sitting on an overstuffed couch in the lobby, waiting. She gave me a big smile. She looked a little thinner and was wearing a fancy outfit with black buttons on her white blouse like a line of insects going up. She came over and awarded me a kiss.

We walked out onto the street. The people who passed looked at us, an odd couple. After a few blocks we chose a little diner, a booth in the back with cracked red plastic upholstery, a sugar shaker with an indented top, a two-sided silver napkin holder that shone.

"I was thinking as I was waiting," she said, "how old you've gotten."

This one almost had me crying immediately, but instead I lifted my water glass and ran my finger round and round the wet circle it left on the table.

"I'm no older than any other sixteen-year-old."

"Yes you are."

"Don't get sappy on me." I had recovered.

"Remember when we took you to church with us that first Christmas. We sat up front and you sat in the back because you didn't know any of the ceremony and were afraid you'd get called on."

"And I fell asleep."

"And when you woke up they were carrying the incense

burner down the aisle toward you and it had gotten dark in the church and you thought they were coming to get you."

"A case of mistaken identity."

We were quiet for a moment.

"Why did you bother to fall in love with Shep when this is how it ends?"

"Shep's ambitions in life were to be good and to be liked. And those were fine ambitions. I didn't know it was going to end. You never know it's going to end."

"Who gets the door knocker?"

She gave a sad smile. "The one on our door with Kean on it? I suppose he does, he's the original Kean."

"No, the one on your bathroom of the two people kissing."

"I have no idea about that one. Ah, but now you admit that they kiss, not hit, when you knock. You can have it."

"They kiss. But probably because they don't know each other very well. If they did, they'd just look at each other real close and then decide to move out on each other."

Terri didn't laugh; she obviously wanted to be serious. I had always thought that she had no illusions about life. She looked relaxed and confident. I remembered my mother saying to me, after I explained to her for the millionth time about Shep and Terri and my visits, "I hope they live up to your expectations."

"You brought a girl with you once when you visited, remember?" Terri said. "A very nice girl, very smart."

"Alixe, yes." Too nice. When all I wanted was to get my hands on her in some faraway place, she just refused. I had been stupid dragging her up to Connecticut when I barely knew her, but I thought magic would happen there. She was in baby arithmetic which should have told me something. But I was excited by her skinny arms and back and wanted things to work out too fast.

"I still feel badly about that weekend," Terri said.

"A loss. But a small loss."

"I mean I monopolized her and probably you wanted to be with her more."

"She liked you." She liked me also, right into the "we'll be friends" conversation. It was true that Terri had kept her away from me for the 30 hours we were there, leaving me with Shep and three kids who wanted to tackle me.

"Well, I wanted to tell her how wonderful you were."

"Thanks. She has a boyfriend now, a wrestler."

"That's long ago I guess," she said. "So tell me about Sara."

"Nothing new," was my answer. I said this because I did not want Terri to know that there was someone else who would see me into the future, who would show me about love changing and about how these changes might even lead to some improvements.

"That's too bad," she said, knowing I was lying, knowing all about me and my life and my secrets. She left it at that.

The rest of the meal (I was hungry and finished two grilled cheeses and a coke), she gave me advice. It wasn't embarrassing to talk about God or to cry. People don't like to hear complaints or apologies. All over the place, like that. It felt girlish and emotional.

Then she said, as we were getting up, "You know, your mother loves you and you should give her a chance."

Which reminded me of one of Billy's favorite expressions: If it doesn't kill you, it will do you good. So I told her that one. Also that I'd consider her suggestion.

I said, "I'll call you."

We hugged and then she walked me back to my car which had a new, quiet air inside when I shut the door.

In the quiet, before I started the engine, I realized why I never asked my mother about my father. I believed that she would have expected something in return, most likely something I could not give her—a bright future, some certainty. The guarantee that I'd tell her, "It's good to see you," every time I saw her.

But mostly I never asked her about my father because she would have been foggy about him. She would have offered no particulars, or maybe just the few stories she had given before. And that would have left me even hungrier. She was, after all, a Sterling only by marriage, stubborn and independent, and she probably wanted her memories of my father for herself. At best, she would have pinned down what she quickly remembered, offering little about my father's heart.

Just yesterday, the geniuses gave me the Prisoner's Dilemma as a throwaway. They were talking about the mathematics of evolution when I wandered by and they were done working on the problem. In the Prisoner's Dilemma, two criminals are captured by the police and given a deal. If they both confess, they both go to jail. If one confesses and the other doesn't, the confessor is set free while his pal heads off to the slammer. If they both keep silent, they're both set free. Confess or keep silent?

For the prisoners, cooperation (that is, silence) would clearly work best. But I believed that logic would lead those involved to confess. It was my life, wasn't it? although it didn't hit me until I was in the car. The Prisoner's Dilemma, over and over: me and Mom, me and Terri, me and Sara. The slammer wasn't the end point for me, but there was a different kind of loss.

Logic didn't work for me; confessing was the hard part. I've always had trouble with it: hopes, fears, plans right out on the table. Even though confessions are supposed to make you feel better, they don't, as any criminal will tell you. At the same time that you're confessing, you're swearing to yourself that you'll never be in this situation again, you'll never repeat this stupid mistake. If I've learned anything, it's that all confessions come in their own time and in their own imperfect way.

I have Sara and a dream of love. There, I said it.

I started thinking, at least for a moment, as I watched Terri walking away, that there were not many things wrong with my life. A more optimistic outlook was in order for a cynic like me on this fine day. My mother could not give me back my father in any way that I didn't already know, and to expect anything different was to have a supreme misunderstanding. She would be with a man, maybe Lester Warner, maybe someone else, convinced that things were destined to go a particular way, but that her certainty was only for herself.

I have Sara, her blast of love only minutes old, and I keep watching for things I can predict.

WITHDRAWN